OLIVER!

by Mary Hastings

Adapted from the screenplay based on Lionel Bart's "Oliver!"
freely adapted from Charles Dickens' "Oliver Twist"

Illustrated with photographs from the motion picture

Random House • New York

OLIVER!

CHAPTER 1

It was one of those incredible days, so crisp and clear that nothing in the English countryside seemed far or near to the eye. The deep snow was new and dazzling and a few miles from Dunstable the thrilling cries of a fox hunt rang out in the clear, quiet air. It was a day for leaping and being glad, and the merry sounds of the hunt seemed appropriate.

Staying close to a hedgerow, an anxious-looking young woman made her way across a snow-covered field. The snow by the hedge was drifted and difficult to walk in, but the girl seemed concerned to stay out of sight. The sound of the hounds baying in the distance frightened her. She started as if she, rather than some bushy-tailed fox, might be the object of the chase. She was obviously poor for she was dressed shabbily. Yet there was something in her thin face—a kind of dignity and grace—that did not seem used to poverty. Her wrists and hands, bare and frost-bitten, clung to a small knotted bundle of belongings. There was an aura of delicacy about her, but she moved cumbersomely and breathlessly for she was enormously heavy with the weight of an unborn child.

Panic stiffened the girl's face as the hunt bore down on the hedgerow from the opposite side. The huntsmen were thick, beefy men warmly clad in britches, fine leather boots, and stylish red hunting jackets. They drove their horses fiercely, whipping and spurring the proud animals to greater efforts; and the hounds bayed raucously, half mad with the excitement of pursuit. Indeed, the entire hunt, which had sounded so gay in the distance, now seemed an insane force as clouds of steamy breath poured forth like dragon smoke from the mouths and nostrils of dogs, horses, and men.

Amid barking and yelling, the crunching of hoofs and paws on the fresh snow drew near to the hedgerow. Worn to the point of collapse, the girl ceased hurrying and huddled down close to the hedge. She cowered there as the yapping hounds burst through the bushes, and horses and men sailed over her head. Horse after horse crashed down behind her and still she crouched motionless in the snow. And then, oblivious of the girl, the hunt was gone. Slowly she stirred and started off again, shakily, dazed with the miracle of being still alive. Except for the trampled snow, the scene was the same as before.

Hours later, in the darkness of evening, the girl was still trudging along a road. Bent forward against the rising wind, she clutched her shawl about her and stumbled on. Mercilessly, the falling snow turned into rain, which fell harder and harder, accompanied from time to time by crackling lightning and thunder. Ahead, warm yellow lights glowed in a small village.

A mail coach clattered down the road, drenching the girl with a filthy mixture of rain and melted snow. Slowly, painfully, she continued on toward the village. And, at last, she was there.

She leaned for support against a huge stone wall, then struggled on for a few more steps until she stood before a gate. It was a high, forbidding structure of iron bars and into the bars was worked a sign, also made of iron. Lit from time to time by flashes of lightning, the sign read: WORKHOUSE – HOME FOR PAUPERS AND ORPHANS. The girl reached up and pulled the bell cord once. Then she crumpled, half-conscious, to the pavement.

From somewhere inside the gates, a fragile, haunted-looking old man appeared and half-carried the exhausted girl inside. The workhouse was built like a fortress or a prison with huge stone walls and bare stone corridors. The windows, where there were any at all, were barred. As the old man dragged the girl through the halls, toothless old paupers peered weirdly out of dark rooms and corners.

From somewhere in the workhouse there came a harsh, stout woman of about forty who was obviously in charge. Her name was Corney—the Widow Corney—and her ancient charges, clearly terrified, disappeared at once from the doorways as she strode brusquely down the corridor. She cast a look of scornful irritation over the half-conscious pregnant girl and, without offering to help the old man, she turned instead to dispatch a particularly sickly old pauper out into the wet night to fetch a doctor.

The girl was taken into a windowless room, lit only by a small

5

candle. An ancient woman in rags entered, lugging a large tub of water which was half her size and twice her weight. The girl, now fully unconscious, was placed on the table. Blanketless and with one grimy sheet, the table had been made up to serve as a bed. The doctor arrived drenched through and through like the quivering pauper who had fetched him and who now ushered him into the room.

"It's another mother," said the Widow Corney with a scowl. "I don't know why they have to throw themselves on me. As if I didn't have enough else on my hands!"

The doctor looked sadly at the young woman on the table and then silenced Widow Corney with a look of fierce scorn. He opened his bag and set about his work. Except for the roaring of thunder outside, the workhouse was silent. From time to time

the ragged pauper woman stretched out her bony hands to offer the doctor wet rags. Long hours passed and then it was done. In the drab room a baby gasped and bellowed out the first sounds of life. Weakly, the young mother on the table stretched out her arms to receive her baby from the doctor. She smiled briefly, kissed the child, and fell back.

The doctor handed the child to Widow Corney and bent urgently over the mother, listening to her chest. From the pauper woman sitting by the tub came the sound of soft weeping.

"Well doctor?" whined Widow Corney impatiently. "What *is* it?"

Utter disgust replaced the deep pity in the doctor's eyes as he glared at Widow Corney. Clearly he hated the workhouse and he was anxious to leave now that his work was done.

"It's a boy," he said finally. "The mother is dead."

And then he left.

As soon as the doctor had gone, Widow Corney became suddenly busy. She placed the baby in the pauper's arms and began fumbling through the young mother's belongings. Finding nothing there of value, she turned to the girl. There was no wedding ring, but the widow's eyes gleamed as she noticed a delicately wrought gold locket and chain about the girl's neck. For a moment she fingered the locket thoughtfully. Then, taking the baby from the pauper, she dismissed the old woman and began bustling about with sudden alacrity.

The locket she slipped hastily into her apron pocket. The orphan boy she carried down the hall to another room marked ORPHAN INFANTS. This room, windowless like the first, was furnished with small, rough wooden boxes which served as cradles. Into such a box Widow Corney deposited the new baby. Then, contentedly patting the pocket that held the locket, she turned away to seek her own more comfortable bed.

CHAPTER 2

The workhouse, with its gaunt old folks and ragamuffin children, took little notice of the new arrival. Though supposedly a charitable institution, it was, as its name implied, a house of work where children too young and men and women too old labored without reward. The rich men of the town boasted of their kindness in sponsoring this haven for the destitute, but they took little interest in its management except to cast their miserly eyes over its accounts lest any money should come out of their own pockets.

Apart from Widow Corney there was only one other salaried

official at the workhouse. He was Mr. Bumble, a petty official of the town with no specific responsibilities. For Mr. Bumble alone the workhouse provided a refuge. A fat, officious man, he was disliked throughout the town and, being uncomfortable in the presence of the rich, he took his heavy staff of office to the workhouse, where he found much pleasure in striking fear into children and old people. One other thing attracted him to the workhouse—the Widow Corney. Between the two there fluttered

a ridiculous and childish flirtation; and Widow Corney, being the shrewder of the two, was pleased to pass on much of her responsibility to her flabby suitor.

So it was that the job of naming the boy, born and orphaned that rainy night, fell to Mr. Bumble. The fat man called him Oliver Twist. When he grew too big for his box cradle, Oliver Twist was moved into a dormitory with the other boys, where he was assigned a hard plank bed. As soon as this happened he was considered old enough to work at the treadmill. Like all of the boys born at the workhouse, Oliver virtually learned to walk at the treadmill. The work was hard and monotonous, but most of the boys labored obediently. Scant food, hard work, and little sleep kept the time and energy for boyish rebellion at a minimum. And regular beatings from Mr. Bumble effectively prevented the children from even considering such antics.

But Oliver Twist was not a rebellious boy by nature. He worked when he had to, ate what little he was given, and slept when he could. He was always tired, but he did not mind his life. To him the workhouse was more than a home—it was his whole world. He knew no other. A kind boy, he was well liked by the few who knew him. But, for the most part, his presence at the workhouse was scarcely noticed. Only troublesome boys were noticed, and Oliver Twist was no trouble at all.

But the hunger was difficult. And it was that never-ending gnawing in the stomach that caused all the trouble.

Once a month from the governors' dining room there drifted smells of glorious food, making the boys sniff and their stomachs rumble. The day when the wealthy made their monthly charity call was hard to bear, for it stirred the boys' imaginations with dreams of a better life. On one such day it was the misfortune of Oliver Twist to be in the wrong place at the wrong time.

For some reason lunch was late and for once the boys had a moment between work and gruel to sniff at the governors' window and to talk among themselves. In a corner of the cobbled yard, Oliver and a few other boys huddled together, whispering excitedly.

Oliver watched with interest as an older boy stooped down and gathered up a handful of straws. The boy turned his back and broke the straws into different lengths. Then he turned around clutching the straws in one hand so that only one end of each straw was visible. Each boy solemnly chose a straw, and then they compared lengths.

"Ha! Ha! Oliver," cried one with relief. "You've got the short one. You have to ask."

Oliver fidgeted with his straw, wishing with all his heart that he had not chosen to enter the game.

"Must I?" he pleaded. "I'm not hungry. Really I'm not."

"If you don't we'll eat your gruel," said the others. "We want more. And if you don't get it for us we'll eat yours."

The boys didn't mean any harm. They had drawn straws fairly and Oliver had chosen the short one. They were just hungry. And so was Oliver Twist.

"All right," he said. "I'll do it."

"Hurray!" cheered the boys. "Hurray for Oliver Twist!"

Just then the lunch bell rang and Mr. Bumble appeared.

"Silence!" he shouted. "Step lively now—and no talking."

The boys, all barefooted, shuffled silently into line and marched into the workhouse. Several of the governors stepped into the hall to watch them pass and Bumble smiled, patting a few of the boys on the head in a sudden display of affection.

As soon as Mr. Bumble had left the eating hall, excitement filled the room. Word of what Oliver was about to do spread

14

quickly and the boys talked and sang of glorious food, gobbling their gruel with abandon until Mr. Bumble returned with the Widow Corney.

"Come on, Oliver," whispered a boy as the stout pair strode to the front of the room.

After much nudging and whispering, Oliver stood. Carrying his wooden bowl and spoon before him like an offering, he

15

marched boldly up to Mr. Bumble and did what no child in the
history of the workhouse had ever done before.

"Please, sir," he said in a small, clear voice. "I want some
more."

"M-o-o-o-o-o-ore!" roared Mr. Bumble.

His face turned crimson, his arms flew up in the air, and he
took a threatening step toward Oliver.

Trembling with fear, Oliver backed a few steps, spun around and fled. Over tables and under benches he scrambled as Bumble mustered various ancient paupers for the chase. Wanting to appear innocent, the other boys rose from their benches and ran after Oliver, too.

"Catch him!" bellowed Bumble.

"Hold him!" screeched Widow Corney.

Oliver leaped from a table to a high window sill. Finding the window barred, he jumped to the floor and rushed up the stairs toward the door. There two old men grabbed him and pinned him to the floor. The room fell silent.

"Got him!" gloated Bumble as he puffed up the stairs. "So

19

it's more you want, is it? Then more you shall have—more cock-roaches to eat, more beatings to keep you warm, and much more trouble than you bargained for."

He took Oliver firmly by the ear and dragged him down the corridor to the governors' dining room. Never had Oliver seen such food as was spread before the governors. Turkey, potatoes, pie, and fine wine covered the fancy white tablecloth; and the fat men laughed and belched luxuriously, their thoughts obviously not on works of charity.

When Mr. Bumble explained breathlessly what Oliver had done, the verdict of the governors was unanimous.

"Such greed!" said a man with gravy on his shirt.

"We've spoiled him," said a fat man, his mouth full.

"Sell the brat," they agreed.

CHAPTER 3

Oliver's departure from the workhouse was prompt and, from the point of view of workhouse routine, insignificant. One boy more or less did not matter. So when Mr. Bumble led him out the door that day there were no good-bys. Nobody even noticed.

But for Oliver, the day was remarkable in several ways. In the first place, he was wearing his first pair of shoes. These did not please him for he had no socks; and the shoes, being several sizes too large, made his feet and ankles raw. Still he had to admit that it was better than walking barefoot in the snow.

The second thing which impressed him was the gate. Never before in the entire nine years of his life had Oliver Twist set foot outside the huge iron gate. Now, as the gate closed behind him, Oliver looked back momentarily. For the first time it occurred to him to wonder whether the gate was meant to keep people in or out. Were the friends he left behind prisoners in the workhouse and was he, Oliver Twist, now free? Or was it the other way around? He did not know. It was simply amazing to be on the other side of that gate.

The fact that he was to be sold did not disturb Oliver in the least. His experience at the workhouse had given him no self-respect, so being sold did not seem an indignity. Indeed, somewhere he harbored half a hope that somehow the transaction would put him in better circumstances. But with only a bit of burlap over his shirtsleeves for warmth, Oliver was soon too cold to keep his mind on such speculations. Carrying his small bundle of belongings, he trudged silently after Mr. Bumble.

It was snowing hard when the two reached the Dunstable Market. Footsore and shivering, Oliver took little notice of the new sights around him. He simply followed obediently the heavy guiding hand of Mr. Bumble, trying, as the fat man ordered, to look healthy and happy.

Here and there was a sign that said APPRENTICE WANTED or BOY NEEDED or HELP WANTED. But, in spite of his efforts to the contrary, Oliver looked so thin and woebegone that when evening came he was still up for sale.

"One boy! Buy a boy!" Mr. Bumble continued to cry. "He's going cheap. Buy a boy."

Some children at play in the street laughed at Oliver and one of them hit him in the back of the neck with a snowball. Oliver's eyes filled with tears, but he did his best to smile as Mr. Bumble

23

commanded.

Then, just before dusk, a small gaunt man appeared in the doorway of a shop marked SOWERBERRY'S FUNERAL HOME.

"How much did you say?" asked the man.

"A mere three pounds, Mr. Sowerberry," cooed Mr. Bumble. "A bargain if ever there was one."

The man beckoned them into the shop. It was a small place

full of coffins and funeral wreaths in various stages of production. Even the dark wooden walls were covered with plans and drawings of coffins. The only bit of color in the shop was a large painting of an elaborate funeral procession, guaranteed to lure even the most poverty-stricken and miserly into lavish spending. A sign on the wall advertised CHEAP FUNERALS.

Over the lid of an unfinished coffin, an evil-looking boy of about eighteen glared at Oliver. His name was Noah Claypole.

"Missus," called Mr. Sowerberry in a small voice. "Here's Mr. Bumble with a boy for sale."

From the back of the shop Mrs. Sowerberry burst through a curtain and peered sharply at Oliver through weasel-like eyes. She was short, stout, and beak-nosed. Her dress, like nearly

everything else in the shop, was basically black. Mr. Bumble shifted uneasily, waiting for a decision.

"Too small," said Mrs. Sowerberry at last.

"Maybe so, Mrs. Sowerberry," wheedled Mr. Bumble. "But he'll grow. I promise you that."

"I daresay he will—on *our* food and *our* drink," she snapped. "Did you really expect us to pay you for the privilege of feeding him? And him too sickly to do a stitch of work? Not likely!"

It looked as if the Sowerberrys were going to turn Oliver away. And, though he didn't know what would happen instead, Oliver was glad to think that he wouldn't be living in such a gloomy place as the funeral shop.

For some time Mr. Sowerberry had been staring at the painting on the wall. Now, suddenly, he spoke up, humbly suggesting that Oliver's mournful face might be a perfect addition to funeral processions. Professional mourners were usual, but a child mourner would be extraordinarily touching! Even Mrs. Sowerberry had to agree that her husband's suggestion was a good one.

"Cash on delivery!" said Mr. Bumble as he held out his hand and began backing toward the door.

"Oh, n-o-o-o, Mr. Bumble!" said Mrs. Sowerberry shrewdly. "Cash upon *liking!* We'll try him out for a week and then decide. Or else you can take him with you right now," she threatened.

It was settled. Oliver would stay on approval. He was to work hard, eat little, and march in funeral processions with a high hat on his head and a sad expression on his face.

All this time Noah Claypole had been peering at Oliver and, when no one was looking, making faces at him. He hadn't said anything, but he stared in such a mean way that Oliver felt afraid.

As soon as Mr. Bumble had gone, Mrs. Sowerberry turned to the boy and said, "Noah, you take charge of Oliver. See that he sweeps up, fills the lamps, and earns his keep."

Noah smiled wickedly at Oliver. "I'll take care of him, Missus. Don't you worry about that," he said.

Noah's idea of taking care of Oliver was to make him as miserable as possible. In the next days, Oliver tried with all his might to please, but Noah seemed bent on interfering with everything he did. When Oliver swept up a pile of sawdust, Noah walked

through it on purpose. When he was filling lamps Noah bumped into him, causing the lamp oil to spill. Oliver, however, said nothing of all this to the Sowerberrys. If he had to be there at all, he was determined to make the best of things.

When he was not working about the shop, picking up after Noah Claypole, Oliver's sad thin face could be seen leading funeral processions. For this work the Sowerberrys fitted him out with a high silk hat and a black suit, complete with tails. The hat was too big, but wads of paper kept it from slipping down over his eyes.

This work was easier than the work at the treadmill, but it was lonelier. And Noah Claypole's sly tricks made Oliver almost wistful for the workhouse.

Strange things indeed were happening inside Oliver Twist. His friends at the workhouse had been a comfort that protected him from the harshness of his life. There, there had been no boys better or worse off than himself. Without them now he found two new feelings welling up painfully within himself. For the first time in his life Oliver knew hatred and loneliness. He hated Noah Claypole. And, though he had never known her, he was lonely for his mother.

Through some demonic sense Noah became aware that Oliver was yearning for his mother almost at the same moment that Oliver knew it himself. Oliver was just bending over to sweep up some sawdust that Noah had intentionally sprinkled on the floor. Suddenly the bigger boy kicked him sharply from behind.

"How's your mother, workhouse boy?" jeered Noah.

Oliver winced. "You leave her out of it," he said bravely. "She's dead."

"What's the matter, Workhouse?" Noah went on. "Does he miss his Mum?"

31

It was too much to bear. In a sudden fury, Oliver swung around with his broom and began beating Noah as hard as he could. When the big boy took away the broom, Oliver picked up the huge wooden mallet that was used in the building of coffins.

"'Elp! 'Elp! Missus Sowerberry!" cried Noah. "'E's murdering me. The new boy's murdering me!"

Inside and outside the shop, Oliver pursued the cowardly bully. Mrs. Sowerberry rushed out, but Oliver turned on her, too.

"Hold the brat!" she screamed. "Don't let him go."

Small though he was, it finally took Noah and Mr. and Mrs. Sowerberry to hold Oliver down. At last they succeeded in shutting him up in one of the coffins. And, while both Sowerberrys sat on the lid of the coffin, Noah ran to fetch Mr. Bumble.

Inside the coffin, Oliver gradually settled down with his hatred and was quiet. All his life he had done what he had been told to do. And in return he had received nothing but gruel, beatings, hard work, and a board to sleep on. Oliver had never known anything better, but suddenly he realized that he could stand no more. Maybe he would starve, but he wasn't going to do one more thing for any Sowerberrys or Claypoles or Bumbles or Corneys. Not one thing.

Mr. Bumble was enjoying a pleasant flirtation with Widow Corney when Noah arrived, screaming that the new boy was about to lay siege to the whole town of Dunstable. Mr. Bumble regretted the interruption and he was not happy with the prospect of having Oliver on his hands again. Still, he followed Noah with alacrity, proud to be needed for once and pleased with the opportunity of lording it over the Sowerberrys.

Brandishing his staff of office, Mr. Bumble entered the Sowerberrys' shop with great bravado. Mr. and Mrs. Sowerberry were still sitting on the coffin lid, which lurched from time to time as Oliver pushed against it with all his might.

"Oliver!" Bumble roared grandly.

"Yes?" said Oliver from inside the coffin.

"You know who this is, Oliver?" asked Bumble.

"Yes."

"And ain't you trembling with fear, Oliver?"

"No, I'm not."

Oliver threw himself against the coffin lid, just as the Sowerberrys leaped off, clutching each other in fear.

"Wa-watch it!" yelped Noah.

"Stand back, everybody," said Mr. Bumble. He waved his heavy staff majestically.

As Oliver emerged stiffly from the coffin, Mr. Bumble grabbed

him with one hand, carefully raising his staff in the other. He
dragged the struggling but exhausted boy across the floor and
shoved him down the basement stairs. From a safe distance
Noah Claypole tossed Oliver's belongings down after him.

"We'll see about you in the morning," said Mr. Bumble as he
locked the door.

But Oliver had no intentions of waiting for morning. Wandering forlornly about the dark basement in search of a way to escape, he startled a mouse which scurried up a wall and disappeared. Oliver looked up and found to his joy that there was a grating. He piled up some old coffins, climbed up, and jiggled the bars. The grating was loose! Quickly he removed it and slipped out into the night, leaving the basement empty of both one mouse and himself.

CHAPTER 4

Just before dawn Oliver managed to slip onto the back of a horse-drawn vegetable wagon. He hid himself in a large bushel of cabbages and waited for several bumpy hours to see where the cart was going. At last the wagon pulled to a halt.

Oliver was just about to peep out of the bushel when the farmer released the catch that allowed the rear of the wagon to tip—spilling cabbages, turnips, Oliver, and all into the street.

Oliver blinked his eyes in the bright morning sun and stared wide-eyed at the sights about him. Flocks of sheep, herds of cattle, and more people than Oliver had ever seen filled the

street—bleating, mooing, and shouting. He was in the rear part of the London market, where farmers came in the early morning to sell their goods to the London shopkeepers. It was here that Oliver would seek his fortune.

"Hey you!" cried the farmer as Oliver got slowly to his feet.

As fast as he could, Oliver ran through the crowds of people and animals. He plunged down an alley and arrived, breathless but safe, in the middle of a busy street of shops. Slowly he climbed some steps and sat down to rest and think out what he should do.

He watched hungrily as vendors peddled their wares from stalls set up on the pavement below him. Then something caught his eye. A boy somewhat older than he was making his way

along the pavement. What fascinated Oliver was the way the boy was dressed. He wore a man's overcoat which was so large that it nearly reached his ankles. The coat was open at the front revealing a garishly colorful vest and striped pants as outsized as the coat. To top off the whole ludicrous outfit, the boy wore a high silk hat. Only by resting it on his ears did he manage to keep it from slipping over his eyes. The sight was so comical that Oliver would have laughed aloud had the boy not moved so gracefully and casually as to be almost inconspicuous in spite of his strange apparel.

With his hands in his pockets the boy wandered in and around the stalls and barrows, stopping at last beside a fruit stall. There he stood momentarily, looking into the air and whistling to himself. Then as the fruitseller turned briefly to help a customer the boy swiftly plucked a couple of plums from the wheelbarrow, whisked them into one of his large pockets, and strolled on casually.

Oliver watched, stunned, as the boy moved on to the next stall. Catching sight of Oliver, the boy stared at him steadily for a moment. Then when the lady at the stall was not looking he whipped up a bun from her counter and slipped it, too, into his pocket. He grinned up at Oliver, who looked away, pretending to notice nothing.

Next the boy sat down just a few steps below Oliver and began eating the bun with relish. Oliver watched hungrily as the bun disappeared. The boy looked up.

"Wotcher starin' at?" he said. "Ain't you never seen a lift?"

"I'm sorry," said Oliver.

"It's all right," said the other. "Don't trouble yourself. Hungry?"

"Well, yes," said Oliver slowly. "It *has* been a while . . ."

"Catch," said the boy.

He tossed Oliver one of the plums and watched, pleased, as Oliver stuffed the whole thing into his mouth.

"Running away from the beak?" said the bigger boy.

"The what?" said Oliver.

"The beak. Don't say you don't know what a beak is?"

"It's a bird's mouth, isn't it?" said Oliver.

"I say, you *are* green!" laughed the older boy. "A beak's a constable! A policeman! Who are you running from then— your old man? Are you running away from home?"

"No, I'm an orphan," said Oliver. "I've come to London to seek my fortune."

The boy moved closer to Oliver and looked at him with interest.

"Oh you have, have you?" he said confidentially. "Got any lodgin's?"

Oliver shook his head.

"I see," said the boy thoughtfully. "Then you'll be needing a place to stay tonight, eh?"

"Do you know of one?" asked Oliver.

"I might do, matie," said the boy. "I might do. I know a re- spectable gentleman what'll give you lodgings for nothing if you've got a proper introduction. And I can take care of that— that is if you'll tell me your name."

"It's Oliver. Oliver Twist."

"And mine's Jack Dawkins," said the boy cheerfully. "Better known among me friends as the Artful Dodger."

"What does that mean?" Oliver asked.

The Dodger looked at him mysteriously for a moment. Then, putting his arm around Oliver, he led him down the steps.

"You'll find out soon enough," he said. "Come on now and

welcome to London. Consider yourself at 'ome!"

Skipping and darting about, the Dodger maneuvered deftly through the wealthier part of London. At first Oliver was bewildered and uncertain. But the merriment was catching, and soon he too was laughing gaily and frisking about the streets like his new friend.

" 'Ome," as the Dodger called it, was located in the poorest part of London. Oliver followed his friend down evil-smelling dark alleys where beggars were trying to sleep, up wooden stairs that shook with age, and across rooftops of rat-infested tenements.

At last, after crossing a footbridge high between two buildings, the Dodger opened a rooftop door and pulled Oliver in after him.

The room in which Oliver found himself was a sort of attic or loft. Like the rest of the neighborhood, it was dilapidated and run-down. Light filtered through a filthy skylight in the roof, revealing dingy wooden walls and a sagging plank floor. Across the room a wide chimney had been broken open to serve as a sort of kitchen. The crevice in the chimney was wide and the bricks removed from it had been carefully piled in one corner, making a small fireplace within the chimney. Clouds of steam billowed energetically from a large kettle above the fire. In another corner of the chimney kitchen hung an assortment of pots, pans, and long forks.

But Oliver scarcely noticed all of this. Instead he stared in astonishment and delight at something else in the room. Lounging about on sacking beds or dangling their feet from the rafters were more than a dozen boys of about his own age or older. They gazed at Oliver with silent interest.

"Evenin' all," said the Dodger. "Where's Fagin?"

A tall, skinny old man peered out of the chimney kitchen. He had a straggling beard and long wild hair, and he wore a long flannel robe that hung loosely about him. His face lit up with pleasure as he saw the Dodger. Oliver sensed that the two must be special friends.

"Here I am, Dodger, my dear," said Fagin.

"I've brought a new lodger—name's Oliver," said the Dodger. "Oliver Twist."

47

The Dodger pushed Oliver forward toward Fagin, who looked at him out of sharp but kindly eyes. The old man bowed ridiculously and offered his bony hand for Oliver to shake.

"How do you do, my dear," he said.

"H-how do you do, sir," said Oliver.

"I hope you'll feel very welcome here, Oliver," said Fagin with a mischievous twinkle in his eyes. "We're very glad to see you, aren't we, my dears?"

At this the boys sprang to life. Dropping from rafters and leaping from corners, they crowded around Oliver, thumping him gladly on the back.

"'Course we are! How are you, Oliver. Welcome!" they chattered.

Fagin whispered quietly with the Dodger and then turned again to the boys, flapping among them like a mad hen.

"Now, get cracking," he ordered. "You there, mind the sausages."

Oliver sat down quietly on a packing case and looked about the loft. Someone tossed him a sausage, which he gulped down with relish. The room was a shambles, very unlike the workhouse which the orphan boys had been forced to keep spotlessly clean. But it was warm and friendly, also unlike the workhouse, and Oliver liked it. He gazed up at the rafters. Between them were stretched yards and yards of string and twine from which hung hundreds of pocket handkerchiefs. Oliver looked at these curiously.

"Is this a laundry, then, sir?" he asked as Fagin sat down beside him.

The boys laughed.

"Not exactly," chuckled Fagin. "We've a better line of business haven't we, boys?"

"I should say so—and how!" came the replies as the boys laughed again.

"Come then, my dears," said Fagin. "Let's show Oliver how we do it. You see, Oliver," he went on, "there's one thing in life that counts—and that's money in the bank. Am I right, boys?"

The boys cheered as Fagin strode over to a chest in a corner of the loft. From it he took out two or three handkerchiefs, a wallet, a watch and chain, a spectacle case, and a snuffbox. All of these he stuffed into the numerous pockets of his tremendous robe and then began strutting about like a proper gentleman.

"Lovely day, ain't it?" he said to one boy. "And the top of the morning to you, kind sir." He tipped his hat to imaginary passers-by and pretended to look into a shop window.

Winking to each other the boys, too, began bustling about, pretending to ignore Fagin altogether. They walked right past him as if in a crowd, and one boy accidentally pushed another into him.

As the pretense went on, a box became a park bench on which Fagin sat to enjoy a view of the imaginary park. Two boys promptly sat down on either side of him and, while one pretended to converse with Fagin, the other whistled and looked away.

Oliver watched all this closely, wondering if it was a game or a play and, if it was a game, what the point of it could be. He was fascinated, but completely mystified.

"All right, boys," said Fagin at last. "The game's over. Let's see how you've managed."

He called all the boys, including Oliver, to a table in the center of the room. Very dramatically he turned each of his many pockets inside out. To Oliver's amazement, they were all entirely empty!

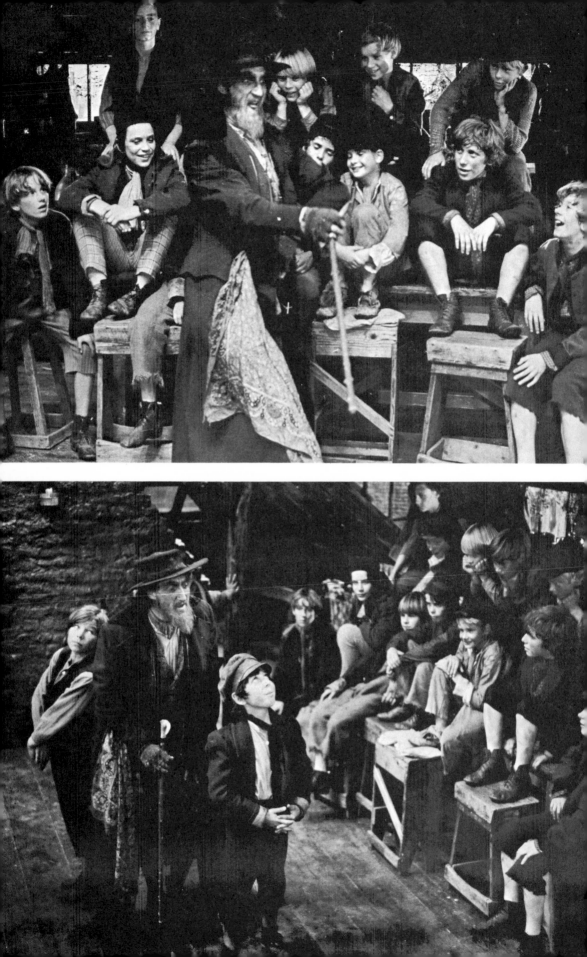

Then, one by one, the boys produced the handkerchiefs, wallet, watch, snuffbox, and spectacle case. Proudly they held them up before Oliver's admiring eyes. So *that* was the game! The boys had taken everything from Fagin's pocket without his or Oliver's noticing at all! Oliver wondered how they had done it—and why!

After everything had been returned to the chest, Fagin held a sort of council.

"Now, then," he said. "I hope you've all been hard at work today, my dears?"

"'Course we have," shouted a boy.

"Good boys—good boys," said Fagin with a twinkle. "Now, Dodger, what have you got to show?"

The Artful Dodger stepped forward and presented Fagin with two wallets. Fagin, in turn, offered them to Oliver for his inspection.

"Nicely made, wouldn't you say, Oliver?"

Oliver studied the wallets. "Yes, sir," he said. "Did the Dodger really make them himself?"

He looked so intently at Fagin, that he was unaware of the boys nudging each other in amusement.

"In a manner of speaking," said Fagin. "And Oliver, you'd like to learn to make wallets like that wouldn't you, my dear?"

"Yes. Yes, sir!" said Oliver.

Another boy turned in a couple of handkerchiefs with embroidered initials in the corners.

"Very nice, my dear," said Fagin. "But you've not done well with the initials. I'm afraid they'll have to be picked out. Oliver," he added. "You'll have to learn to do that, too, won't you, my dear?"

"Yes, sir," said Oliver, "if you'll teach me how."

This time the boys could not hide their laughter. Oliver looked at them in bewilderment, but Fagin put a hand up for silence.

"Of course, I'll teach you, my dear," he said to Oliver. "And so will the Dodger. You do just as the Dodger does. He's a regular little Bill Sikes, he is." He ruffled the Dodger's hair affectionately.

"Who is Bill Sikes?" asked Oliver.

"A very clever gentleman," answered Fagin. "Maybe you'll meet him tomorrow. But now let's have another little game, shall we? Are you ready for your first lesson?"

Oliver watched eagerly as Fagin walked toward the fireplace. He did something with his hands which Oliver could not see. Then suddenly he spun around and peered intently at Oliver.

"Tell me, my dear," he said. "Is my handkerchief protruding from my pocket?"

Oliver looked closely. "Yes, sir," he said. "I can just see the corner."

"Very good, my dear!" said Fagin. "Now, see if you can take it out without my feeling anything—just as you saw the others do."

Once again Fagin began strutting about the room, humming to himself. Oliver followed. He got nearer and nearer to Fagin. It didn't seem hard. In fact, he thought it ought to be very easy. He reached out his hand toward the pocket. Then, just when he thought he could grasp the handkerchief, Fagin spun around so that the pocket was out of reach. The boys snickered, but Oliver tried again. Again and again he got close to the handkerchief. But every time, just when he thought he had Fagin fooled, the old man turned and Oliver had to begin again. The more he tried, the more the boys laughed. Oliver began to feel foolish. He was on the verge of giving up when Fagin failed to turn and, as gently as he could, Oliver plucked the handkerchief away. It was almost too easy and Oliver wondered if Fagin had intentionally let him succeed. But the old man wiped away his doubts.

"Is it gone?" said Fagin with apparent astonishment.

"Yes, sir!" said Oliver triumphantly. He held up the handkerchief proudly.

"Well, imagine that!" Fagin patted Oliver on the head. "You're a clever boy, my dear—never saw a sharper lad."

There was much grumbling and protesting as Fagin herded the boys off to their beds on the floor. But Oliver could see that

all of the boys loved the odd old man.

"Where shall I sleep, sir?" he asked at last.

Fagin led Oliver to a corner near the fireplace. With a flourish he arranged some sacks in a heap on the floor, clowning as though he were making up a real bed.

"A nice cozy bed by the fire," he said. "You'll be lovely and warm here and tomorrow we'll play some more games, eh?"

"Yes, sir. Thank you, sir," said Oliver.

"Sweet dreams, my dear," said Fagin. "Sweet dreams."

From his sacking bed, Oliver watched as Fagin crept about the room. He blew out all of the candles but one. Then, singing a peculiar lullaby about money, he slipped out the door. He was a strange old man, Oliver thought. Indeed, nearly everything about his new home seemed strange. There was something almost mysterious about it. But it was friendly and welcoming, and Oliver liked it. He felt happier than he had ever been in his life.

CHAPTER 5

If Oliver had followed Fagin that night instead of sleeping, he might have felt less happy about his new home and companions. After crossing the rooftop bridge and going down the stairs, Fagin made his way through the dark streets to a tavern called the Inn of the Three Cripples. Inside, a rough-looking crowd laughed and sang raucously accompanied by a tinny-sounding piano. At a table on the balcony sat a young woman. Although her hair was unkempt and her clothes shabby, she was rather pretty. But, for the moment, she appeared forlorn and desperately worried. With her sat a girl of about sixteen, who was clearly concerned about the older one's unhappiness. Fagin joined them, merrily ignoring their gloomy mood.

"Well, if it isn't my two favorite young ladies," he said. "Hello, Nance," he greeted the older girl. "Hello, Bet," he said to the other.

He squeezed in between them and, after looking cautiously about, whispered to Nancy. "Where is he? Where's Bill Sikes?"

"You mean, 'where's the loot?' don't you?" said Nancy with a hard look. "That's all you care about. You send him—you send them all—out to steal for you! They risk their lives, but all you care about is the loot!"

"Not back yet, eh?" said Fagin sympathetically.

Nancy shook her head sadly.

"Well, don't be worrying, Nance," soothed Fagin. "Nothing could go wrong with your Bill on the job—you know that."

Just then from outside in the street came the sound of a dog barking. Fagin grinned as Nancy sat up quickly in her chair and looked toward the tavern door. A terrier-bulldog-like mutt appeared in the doorway, barked once, and disappeared.

"It's Bullseye!" said Nancy. "Bill's dog. Maybe he's all right after all."

She grabbed Bet's hand and headed for the door. Fagin followed, rubbing his hands together excitedly.

Outside, across the street, Bullseye stood waiting at the entrance to a small alley. Rushing after the mongrel, the three headed into the alley. There, slouching against a wall, stood Bill Sikes. He was a tough, evil-looking man with a mean look in his eye. Nancy hurried to his side, her face full of affection and relief. She did not seem disturbed that Bill ignored her.

From under his coat Fagin pulled out an empty sack which he held open in front of Bill.

"All right," he said. "The game. What did you bring me this time, my dear?"

Sikes grumbled and began fishing things out from various deep pockets. Fagin's eyes sparkled as Bill produced an enormous amount of jewelry, fine silverware, and precious stones.

"Beautiful! What a lovely piece that is!" chortled Fagin as Bill placed valuable after valuable into his sack. "You've done well this time, Bill. Real well," he said.

"Come on, come on," said Bill menacingly. He held his giant hand out toward Fagin, wiggling his fingers. "Where's the money?"

Fagin, obviously terrified of physical violence, trembled momentarily. Then, regaining his calm, he spoke soothingly to the strong man before him.

"I couldn't carry gold around at this time of night, not with

59

all the thieves and robbers on the prowl. You know that, Bill," he said. "Come by tomorrow. I'll have the money ready then, I promise."

Bill glowered and Fagin turned hastily to Nancy for help. "Nancy, my dear," he said. "Would you take Bill home and put him to bed."

For a moment Bill glared fiercely at Fagin. Then, shrugging his shoulders, he turned and slouched off down the street with Bullseye at his heels. Nancy whispered good night to Bet and hurried after Bill, while Fagin, struggling under the weight of the sack, tiptoed toward home.

This game was not unlike the one Oliver had witnessed earlier at Fagin's. But this time it was deadly serious. The game was robbery.

Back at Fagin's loft, Oliver slept—peacefully dreaming of nothing—until the sound of Fagin chuckling to himself disturbed him. Oliver blinked himself awake and watched as Fagin shuffled stealthily across the room and emptied his sack on the one candle-lit table. He lit two more candles and began inspecting each of his treasures. Diamonds and silver sparkled in the candlelight, making Oliver's eyes grow wide with wonder.

"It's lovely," Fagin muttered under his breath. "Lovely swag —simply lovely!"

He rose and crept to the fireplace near Oliver. Kneeling down, he raised a loose floorboard and removed a large wooden box or chest bound sturdily with metal bands. Oliver could see that the chest was heavy as Fagin laboriously lugged it back to the table.

The old man sat down at the table and opened the box. Out of it he raised a huge gold watch and chain, which he proceeded to swing back and forth in front of his face.

"Tick tock, lovely watch," he cooed. His eyes moved back and forth following the watch as if he were hypnotized.

Then suddenly he plunged his hands into the chest and began sifting piles of diamond, pearl, and emerald jewelry through his long fingers.

"And it's mine—all mine," he gloated. "Nobody can take my secret treasure from me. It will keep me when I'm old. After all, somebody's got to look after me, haven't they?"

He looked about the room full of sleeping boys. "Will *you?*" he asked. "Will *you* look after your old Fagin?"

Suddenly his eyes fell on Oliver who had propped himself upon one elbow and was staring at the old man in amazement. He slammed down the lid of the box, jumped to his feet, and hurried over to the boy. Terrified by the angry look on Fagin's face, Oliver sat up.

"You're awake!" said Fagin in a sharp voice. "Why are you watching me? What did you see? Quick, now," he demanded. "What did you see?"

"I'm sorry if I disturbed you, sir," said Oliver nervously.

"Were you awake when I came in?" snapped Fagin.

"No, sir."

"Are you sure?"

"Yes, sir. Quite sure," said Oliver.

Slowly Fagin seemed to relax. He patted Oliver gently on the head. "Ah, yes," he said. "I knew that all along, my dear."

He rubbed his hands together, chuckling and looking uneasily over his shoulder at the box on the table. Crossing to it, he put his hand on the box and questioned Oliver again.

"Did you see any of the pretty things in this box, my dear?" he asked.

Seeing that Fagin was calm once more, Oliver spoke up with honest admiration.

"Yes, sir!" he said.

"Well, they're mine!" hissed Fagin fiercely. "It's all I have to live on in my old age!"

He returned to Oliver and whispered confidentially.

"Some people say I'm a miser," he said. "But it's a terrible thing, old age, Oliver. And I'll need my secret treasure then."

Oliver did not understand the old man at all.

"Can I go to sleep again, sir?" he asked.

"Yes, that's right," said Fagin soothingly. "You go to sleep. Old Fagin won't disturb you again. Sleep now, it's all been a dream, my dear."

Obediently, Oliver closed his eyes. He pretended to sleep, but nearly frantic with fright and confusion, he remained wide awake. So much had happened that he could not understand. He thought about the Dodger stealing plums and buns in his gigantic coat. He thought of the handkerchiefs hanging about the room, and of the peculiar pocket-picking game he had learned earlier.

And what of Fagin? Fagin was the greatest mystery of all—

so kind one minute, and so furious the next. The place was not a workhouse and yet it was not possible for Fagin to be the father of all of the boys. Why then had this strange, shabby man taken in so many boys? Why did he want Oliver? And was he rich? There was something about it all that seemed dishonest and disturbing to Oliver. But he thought again of the welcome he had received—the food and the friendliness—and, gradually, he went back to sleep.

CHAPTER 6

The morning sun gave a dusty glow to the skylight in Oliver's new home, gently nudging Fagin's enormous family out of bed. Not far away in another rooftop room, Nancy, Bill Sikes, and the dog Bullseye also stirred and began to wake up. Their room was much smaller than Fagin's den and, thanks to Nancy, somewhat tidier. The only clutter in their little home consisted of the tools of Bill's dishonest trade. On the floor beside the bed lay a jumble of crowbars, wrenches, wires, and coiled rope.

Nancy was the first one to wake up. She crept quietly out of bed, trying not to wake Bill, and busied herself about the stove.

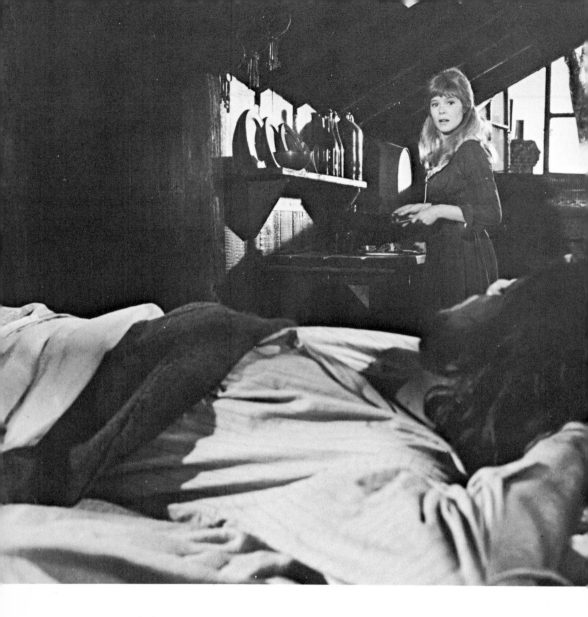

While she made coffee and breakfast, she sang softly of her love for Bill.

"Bill," she called at last. "Breakfast is ready."

"Aw, be quiet, can't you," growled Bill. "Can't you let a man sleep?"

"Sure, Bill," said Nancy sweetly. "I'll warm it up for you later."

"Get over to Fagin's and pick up my money," said Bill.

He rolled over and went back to sleep. Nancy pulled a shawl about her, picked up a basket, and bent lovingly over the sleeping man.

"Bill," she whispered. "I love you. I just wish you didn't have to steal."

Outside, the sun was shining on the dingy streets. Bet sat on the steps in front of the house where Bill and Nancy lived, waiting eagerly for Nancy to come out. When she did, Bet sprang to her feet with an admiring grin on her face.

"Hi, Nancy," she said.

"There's my girl," said Nancy.

As the two girls strolled down the street Nancy chatted casually about her troubles. She led a hard life and in some ways Bill was the worst of it. She cared so much for him and gave so much while he, surly and mean, offered nothing in return. He showed more concern over Bullseye than Nancy and, sometimes, Bet knew, he even beat her. Yet Nancy did not see her life as being a harsh one.

"We ain't rich," she said, "but we've got enough. We've got enough to eat mostly, a place to sleep, good friends and love. And I've got my Bill. He needs me more than he knows. And as long as I've got someone to love and care for, I say it's a fine, fine life."

The two girls walked proudly and briskly in the sun, nodding to friends, and laughing gaily. Passers-by, rich and poor alike, found their good humor infectious and Nancy and Bet left a trail of smiling faces behind them.

After stopping to buy sweet buns for the boys, the girls arrived at Fagin's den. Oliver was seated at the table, gratefully sharing a hot breakfast of toast, sausages, and coffee with the other boys. It was the best breakfast he had ever eaten and with good food before him he was finding it easy to forget the mysterious events of the previous night.

"Ah! Here are the ladies," said Fagin grandly as Nancy and Bet entered. "Come in, my dears!"

"Listen to the old man trying to act like a gent," chided the Dodger.

"That'll be enough from you, young Dodger," said Nancy. She took a good-natured swing at the Dodger's head and began passing out sweet buns to the boys.

At the workhouse Oliver had had many a painful lesson on the proper respect to be shown to elders and now, as he watched the Dodger mimicking Fagin, he found it difficult to laugh with the other boys. Fagin was different from any elder he had known, and Oliver could see that the old man actually enjoyed the Dodger's antics. Still, the easy familiarity between the two made Oliver uncomfortable. To him it seemed disrespectful.

So when Fagin, with mock formality, presented Oliver to Nancy and Bet as a "new member of the establishment," Oliver remained solemn and respectful.

Bowing politely he said, "How do you do?" to the two girls.

Nancy and Bet winked at each other and curtsied elaborately, making the boys hoot with laughter. Oliver glared at them, hurt and angry, but Nancy quickly took his side.

"Don't take any notice of them, Oliver," she said. "Just because you know your manners and they don't."

"What do you mean?" the Dodger interrupted. "I know me manners. I'm a regular gent, I am."

He swept off his hat and bowed low. "Your humble servant, ma'am. Allow me to escort you across the road."

Nancy picked up her skirts and began good-naturedly to join in the fun. She allowed the Dodger to take her hand and lead her across an imaginary puddle.

"And don't let your petticoats dangle in the mud, my darling," he said.

The sight was too much even for Oliver. Nancy and the Dodger, who was at best half her size, made a ridiculous couple. With raised eyebrows and noses in the air, they paraded about the room in a perfect imitation of the rich. The other boys, too, began to join in the fun, bowing, curtsying, and acting like fine gentlemen. It was irresistible. At long last, Oliver Twist began to laugh, too.

The clowning ended abruptly when Nancy caught the Dodger sneaking her purse out of her basket. She slapped his hand and he promptly dropped the purse back into the basket.

"Thank *you,* kind sir!" said Nancy sarcastically. She knocked off his hat and as he bent to retrieve it Fagin kicked him hard from behind.

"What's that for?" howled the Dodger.

"For getting caught," said Fagin.

"Aw go on," said the Dodger, feigning innocence. "I was only practicing. You know I'd have given it back."

Here was the old game again. Oliver continued to laugh with the others, but he was secretly shocked at what he had seen. He didn't really believe the Dodger would have returned the purse if he hadn't been caught.

Nancy took Fagin aside to a corner near the fireplace.

"All right," she said, "hand over. Bill's waiting for his money."

The old miser hemmed and hawed, reluctant to part with even a single penny. He tried charm and excuses, but Nancy stood her ground firmly. At last Fagin slipped a hand into his robe and fished out a leather bag that hung about his neck. Turning his back, he reached into the bag and counted out some coins.

"Aah!" he grumbled. "All he ever thinks about is money."

"That makes two of you then," Nancy said lightly. "Now then, hand over. Or would you rather have Bill come to collect it himself?"

Fagin shuddered, obviously terrified of Bill's violent temper. With a shrug of self-pity, he handed Nancy some money.

"Take it, then!" he grumbled. "Who cares if I starve?"

Meanwhile Oliver watched admiringly as the boys prepared to leave for what they called their "work." He thought of the

beautiful wallets that the Dodger had brought in the day before,
and was eager to learn to make them as Fagin had promised he
could. Walking over to the Dodger, he asked humbly if he could
go along.

"Hey, Fagin," said the Dodger. "Young Oliver wants to work
with us today."

"Eh? What's that?" said the old man. "On the job, you mean?"

"May I, sir?" pleaded Oliver. "I'd like to help."

"Yes, you can go," said Fagin after a pause. "Good luck on
your first job, my dear. Make lots of wallets and handkerchiefs,

73

and I'll be waiting for you when you come back."

The boys giggled, but Oliver was too excited to mind. Thrilled to be a part of things, he followed the boys out the door. They crossed the rooftop bridge and thundered down the stairs to the street, where they split up into small groups of twos and threes. Oliver was to go with the Dodger and a boy named Charlie Bates, but he hesitated a moment in order to wave good-by to Fagin, who was standing on the bridge. The old man waved back affectionately and Oliver, brimming with happiness, hurried after his new friends.

CHAPTER 7

It was still early as Oliver, the Dodger, and Charlie Bates sauntered through the back streets of London on their way to work. But already the streets were crowded with workers, hurrying to and fro in a frenzy of enterprising activity. The doors of warehouses were flung open, allowing much business to be carried on in the streets and alleys.

Butchers in blood-stained aprons chopped away at huge sides of beef. Newspaper boys waving the morning paper charged about in frantic competition with each other. Buttermaids churned, chimney sweepers swept, and bottle washers washed. To

Oliver it all seemed a sort of wonderful dance. Everyone had somewhere to go and something to do. And Oliver was grateful that he, too, had a purpose to carry out.

For a while the boys stood and watched a street circus. Accompanied by the *oom-boop-boop* of a half-empty carousel, two acrobats tossed each other about skillfully. Oliver clenched his fists in sympathy as a gigantic man grunted and raised an enormous dumbbell. He gasped as a man with a beard tipped back his head and swallowed the flames of a blazing torch, while still another opened his throat to receive the entire blade of a two-foot-long sword.

A horse-drawn omnibus clattered past and, following the example of the Dodger and Charlie, Oliver mounted the back for a free ride. For a while they clung undetected to the back of the bus, but then an irate passenger poked at them with an umbrella and they had to flee.

It was nearly noon when the three boys found themselves in a wealthy part of London called Clerkenwell. The mood here was different and more gracious. Fine ladies and gentlemen paraded in and out of shops, greeting each other with much raising of hats, bowing, and curtsying. Oliver smiled as he remembered the clowning that had gone on that very morning in Fagin's den.

He followed the Dodger and Charlie down the street, sticking his hands in his pockets and trying to appear as casual and un-

impressed as they did. But he did not feel casual in the least. Drapery, bakery, grocery, and china shops lined the street, their windows full of beautiful and delicious goods such as Oliver had never imagined.

The three boys lingered hungrily before the bakery window. Inside, an enormous woman stared haughtily back as if daring the urchin trio to enter. Oliver was shocked when his two companions mimicked her expression disrespectfully and went off laughing. But, hanging back at the window, he was struck by their perfect imitation of the woman. And, with a sudden giggle, he hurried after his friends.

He found them standing in the doorway of a shop, carefully watching something across the street.

"How 'bout it, Charlie?" asked the Dodger.

Oliver followed their gaze. Across the street was a bookshop and in front of it, studying a book from an outside display case, stood a tall gray-haired gentleman in fancy clothes. He wore a gray top hat, a green coat with a black-velvet collar, and tailored white trousers.

"Well, Charlie?" asked the Dodger again.

"He'll do," said Charlie with a nod.

The two boys sauntered across the street. After a moment's hesitation Oliver followed, watching closely, a puzzled expression on his face. The Dodger and Charlie stopped on the other side of the street just a few yards from the bookshop. They winked significantly at each other and then strolled along the pavement until they stood directly behind the elderly gentleman. The man continued reading while, much to Oliver's horror, the Dodger raised the green coattail and swiftly removed the wallet from the man's hip pocket.

Feeling the movement of his coattail, the man looked up

from his book and put a hand to his pocket. It was only as the man himself discovered that his wallet was missing that Oliver fully understood what was happening. In one terrible split second everything became clear to him. The wallets that the Dodger had supposedly made were stolen, just like the plums and bun from the market. The handkerchiefs, too, had been stolen and the initials were to be picked out so that Fagin could sell them as new ones. All of Fagin's boys were pickpockets! And Bill Sikes, the shining example, must be a real thief who stole silver and jewels and all the other valuable things that Fagin kept in his secret box. Utterly horrified, Oliver realized that he, too, was expected to steal!

He stood stunned for a moment as he tried to take all this in. Then looking up, he suddenly became aware that the Dodger and Charlie had disappeared. The man in the green coat spun around just as Oliver gathered his wits and began to run.

"Stop! Stop, thief!" called the man, pointing at Oliver.

At once several other gentlemen took up the cry and a dozen or so others began chasing the frightened boy.

In complete panic, Oliver struggled through the crowd, dodging the many hands that reached out to block his way. As he ran past an alley he caught sight of the Dodger and Charlie. With a sense of relief he started toward them. They would help, he was sure. But just then Charlie, too, cried, "Stop, thief!" and the two boys sprang out of the alley toward Oliver.

Oliver's heart sank at this betrayal. But then, as he stumbled over a cobblestone, he saw the Dodger bend to tie his shoe, causing several men to trip and fall. Oliver understood. They *were* trying to help, but there was no sense in all three of them being caught. Over his shoulder he saw Charlie trying to mislead the crowd by yelling "Stop, thief!" again and running off in the

wrong direction.

But all efforts to help were useless. The boys managed to mislead a few men, but the main body of Oliver's pursuers remained close behind him and ahead more stood ready to pick up the chase when others tired.

Then, suddenly, Oliver thought he saw a way to escape. He ducked quickly into a shopping arcade. Panting and gasping for air, he huddled in a doorway and looked back toward the street. His pursuers ran by, unaware that their quarry was not ahead somewhere in the crowd. He had fooled them! But Oliver knew he was not safe yet. In a moment they would discover their error and be back, looking for him in the arcade. Frantically, Oliver searched for a new escape route.

He spotted an alley that connected the arcade with another street! If he could just get through it before the crowd discovered him, he would lose himself in a different throng of shoppers. So far no one was behind him. In a moment he would be safe.

Glancing over his shoulder, Oliver saw with relief that there was still no one following. Now at last he could relax—but not for long. Nearly overcome with exhaustion he stumbled down

the last few steps only to find that he had run in a circle and was back in front of the bookshop. Standing there and talking excitedly with a constable was the gentleman in the green coat! Before Oliver could turn, the man looked up and shouted, "There he is! That's the boy!"

Unable to run another step, Oliver was quickly pinned to the ground by a hefty workman. Angry-faced ladies and gentlemen bent over him accusingly. He did not struggle as the constable pulled him to his feet and presented him to the man in the green coat.

"Is this the thief, Mr. Brownlow?" asked the constable. "Do you identify this boy as the one that stole your wallet?"

"Well," said Mr. Brownlow. "He *is* the boy I saw running away, and——"

"That's enough for me," interrupted the constable. "Come on young feller, let's see how you like spending the night in the lock-up. And tomorrow," he added, "we'll have you up in court before the magistrate."

As the constable dragged him away, Oliver caught sight of the Dodger and Charlie Bates hard at "work" in the dwindling crowd. But he said nothing to the constable about them. They had been good to him and they had tried to help. He wouldn't say anything to anyone about what he had seen.

CHAPTER 8

That night, while Oliver tried in vain to sleep in the cold prison, Fagin, Bet, and Bill sat at their usual balcony table in the Inn of the Three Cripples. Below, a concertina, a harmonica, and an off-key banjo struck up a tune with the tinny piano. A rowdy, gruff cheer rose from the customers as Nancy mounted the piano to entertain them with a song.

"Oom pah pah! Oom pah pah!" she sang gaily.

The men laughed and joined in the song, and one of them tried to dance with Nancy. Bill Sikes's face grew red with rage as he watched. Though he never had even a kind word for

Nancy, he couldn't stand for anyone else to be friendly toward her either.

"Why, Bill!" teased Fagin. "You aren't jealous, are you?"

Bill grabbed Fagin by the throat and shook him violently. The old man's eyes bulged with fear.

"You miserable old skinflint!" roared Bill. "I'll——"

But just then Charlie Bates and the Dodger stumbled through the doorway of the inn. Panting hard, they looked anxiously about and, after spotting Fagin in the balcony, began pushing their way through the crowd.

"They've got him!" said the Dodger as he reached Fagin's table. "They've nabbed Oliver!"

"Shut up and talk sense," snapped Fagin. "What do you mean, 'they've got Oliver?' Who's got Oliver?"

"The beaks!" cried Charlie Bates. "Oliver went and got himself hooked by the beak!"

Together the Dodger and Charlie explained what had happened and how they hadn't known until it was too late that Oliver wasn't with them. They told of the chase and how they had tried in vain to help. Oliver had done well, they said. He was a good sport. They had watched him after his capture and he hadn't breathed a word to the constable about what had really happened.

"'E ain't half bad, Fagin!" exclaimed Charlie. "He just let them haul him away and he didn't peach. And us standin' right there in plain sight!"

Now, however, Oliver was in jail and the two boys were worried about what he might say in court in the morning.

"Blimey, Fagin!" concluded the Dodger. "I think he really believed we were going to teach him to *make* wallets!"

Fagin, who was still trembling over the episode with Bill

Sikes, now turned so pale with fright that he almost looked sick. He shook his fist at the two boys.

"I told you to take care of him," he hissed. "You knew he was green."

All this time Bill sat watching Fagin with amusement. As slow-witted as he was tough, he was thoroughly enjoying the old man's discomfort. And he certainly wasn't worried about Oliver.

"Aah, so what!" he said at last. "What's it matter if the kid does go to jail?"

Fagin looked hard at Bill. "If you weren't so stupid, you'd be worrying too—and plenty. Now listen——"

Fagin proceeded to point out that all members of what he called his establishment were dependent on one another. He, Fagin, was dependent on Sikes and the boys to steal for him. And they, in turn, needed him to sell what they stole in exchange for money.

"You can't buy food with a bunch of wipes now, can you?" he said. "The way things work out the boys here get a home as their reward. And you get a living, right? And all I get is a little something for me old age. But," he said sternly. "We also need each other for something else, don't we, my dear?"

Bill looked on dumbly.

"What about protection!" shouted Fagin. "None of us is going to get nothing if we wind up in jail. And that's exactly what's going to happen if even one of us talks."

He waggled one of his long fingers in Bill's face.

"And it might come out rather worse for you than for any of the rest of us, my dear Bill," he said.

At last it dawned on the stupid man that Oliver's capture could mean trouble for him, too. Humiliated by his own slowness and terrified of the danger, Bill flew into a rage, grabbing Fagin again by the throat.

"Now listen," he growled. "You get yourself down to that court in the morning and find out what happens."

He released Fagin and flung him back into his chair.

"Me? Go to court?" gasped Fagin. "Are you crazy? With the magistrate sitting right there in the same room?"

If there was one thing that frightened Fagin more than violence, it was the law. Even Bill, when he thought about it, had to agree that Fagin couldn't pull off a trip to court. In the presence of a magistrate, the old man would give himself away just by his trembling. But who could go then? Somebody had to.

Nancy had joined the group and was listening carefully to the conversation. Now, putting her hand on Bill's arm, she spoke softly.

"I'll go, Bill," she said.

Fagin's face brightened with relief.

"That's right, my dear," he said. "You come around first thing in the morning, and I'll have some nice clothes all ready for you. Then, if he does talk, you come and tell us quick, eh, Nancy? Because then we'll have to look after ourselves."

"If the kid blabs," threatened Bill, "you won't have to look after anything. But I'll look after you—I promise you that."

CHAPTER 9

As the constable had promised, and as Fagin had feared, Oliver did indeed appear in court the next morning. He was placed in the dock, a sort of wooden pen guarded by two constables. He did not see Nancy, but she was there. Taking care to conceal her face with a shawl, she slipped in and sat with the other onlookers behind a wooden barrier at the back of the courtroom.

The magistrate, a skinny, bad-tempered man, entered and took his place at the front of the court. Peering near-sightedly over his glasses, he signaled to a clerk, who brought Mr. Brown-low to the magistrate's desk.

"And what crime is this fellow charged with?" demanded the magistrate. "He looks a perfect scoundrel."

Mr. Brownlow looked outraged.

"He's not charged at all, your worship," said the clerk. "This gentleman, Mr. Brownlow, is the plaintiff. He is appearing *against* the boy."

Laughter rippled through the courtroom.

"Boy?" snapped the magistrate. "What boy?"

"The boy in the dock, your worship," said the clerk.

"Well stand up, boy!" said the magistrate. "I can't see you!"

"He *is* standing, your worship," said one of the constables.

Again the court laughed. Ten minutes passed and still the magistrate was unable to ascertain either who was on trial or what for. He called upon one person after another, impatiently interrupting each one and then misinterpreting what had been said. Mr. Brownlow grew angrier and angrier at the magistrate's impossible behavior.

"What are we waiting for?" shouted the magistrate at last. "Brownly, or whatever your name is, *will* you state your complaint against this boy or not?"

Carefully controlling his temper, Mr. Brownlow began to speak softly.

"My name, sir, is Brownlow," he said. "Yesterday afternoon I was standing at a bookstall when ——."

"Yes, yes," said the magistrate. "Never mind that."

He turned to Oliver, who stood in the dock, pale with fear and lack of sleep.

"What's your name, boy?" he said.

"Oliver," said Oliver in a small whisper.

"I can't *hear* you!" bellowed the magistrate.

The constable at the dock bent down and listened to Oliver.

"He says his name is Oliver Twist, sir," he reported.

The constable continued to relay Oliver's whispered answers to the magistrate. No, the boy had no parents. Yes, he was an orphan. The magistrate asked where Oliver lived. At the back of the courtroom Nancy leaned forward in her seat and watched anxiously as the constable questioned Oliver.

"He don't seem to be able to say where he lives, nor anything else, sir," reported the constable.

Nancy relaxed against her bench with a sigh of relief.

"Well," said the magistrate. "He's a liar and a thief and an

insolent beggar as well. The boy is committed to prison for three months' hard labor. Clear the court!"

Unable to control his anger any longer, Mr. Brownlow thumped his walking stick on the courtroom floor.

"Upon my soul!" he cried. "This is disgraceful. I demand to be heard."

But just then a man burst into the court, announcing that his name was Jessop and that he was the owner of the bookstore where the crime had occurred.

"Wait!" he cried. "Don't take the boy away!"

"Clear the court!" repeated the magistrate.

"NO!" shouted Jessop. "I saw what happened. Two other boys stole Mr. Brownlow's wallet. This boy had nothing to do with it."

He explained that he had only just heard about the trial and had rushed right over. In spite of the magistrate's protestations, he continued explaining that Mr. Brownlow had been reading a book outside his shop when . . .

"Book?" interrupted the magistrate. "What book? Has he paid for it?"

Mr. Jessop grinned. "Not yet," he said, "but I know Mr. Brownlow well——"

"Dear me!" said Mr. Brownlow. "I forgot all about it!"

"Ah ha!" cried the magistrate. "A fine fellow you are, preferring charges on a poor innocent orphan. Forgot to pay, indeed!"

Mr. Brownlow opened his mouth to protest, but the magistrate would hear no more. "Hold your tongue!" he said. "The boy is discharged. *Clear the court!*"

In utter disgust Mr. Brownlow stamped his foot and cracked his walking stick in two over his knee.

Outside the court a carriage drawn by two horses stood waiting at the curb. Oliver came slowly through the courtroom door, looking dazed and bewildered. Where would he go now, he wondered. Should he go back to Fagin's? And if he did, how would he find his way? And if he found his way, would he then have to become a thief?

Mr. Brownlow, still spluttering, came hurrying out with Mr. Jessop. He hurried over to Oliver.

"My poor boy," he said. "I can never forgive myself for my stupidity."

"It was my fault for running away, sir," said Oliver.

But Mr. Brownlow was determined to make amends. He bade good-by to Mr. Jessop, promising to pay for the book shortly. Then, putting his arm around Oliver, he led him to the horse-drawn carriage at the curb.

"Come now," he said cheerfully. "In you get!"

"But, sir," said Oliver. "Where are we going?"

"Home," said the gentleman.

CHAPTER 10

Bill Sikes did not receive Nancy's news of the court session with pleasure. He was, in fact, furious. The group had assembled in Fagin's den. Bill, Nancy, and Fagin sat at the table, and the boys listened intently to Nancy's story from their places among the rafters and on the floor. When she had finished, Bill rose to his feet, whacking the table with his fist.

"What's the matter with you!" he said. "Why didn't you bring him back?"

This time it was Fagin's turn to be amused. He watched with delight as Bill fussed and fumed about Oliver. Even if the boy

hadn't talked in court, he would speak up sooner or later, Bill said. And now they didn't even know where Oliver was. How could they find him? Sooner or later that boy was going to send the whole lot of them to prison.

To Fagin it was an unusual privilege to see Bill Sikes squirm. But realizing that Nancy had had enough, he intervened at last.

"Take it easy, Bill," he said. "Nancy did the best she could and now all we've got to do is bring sweet little Oliver back home."

"And just how are we going to do that?" said Bill. "He went in a carriage, didn't he? And we don't know where, do we?"

Fagin chuckled to himself, shaking his head with glee.

"You think old Fagin was born yesterday?" he said. "You think I got no brains in my head?"

Putting a long finger on Bill's chest, he pushed the big man aside and strolled over to the Dodger.

"Dodger?" he said. "When you pinched the wallet, the gent was standing outside a bookshop, right?"

"I told you—in Mutton Lane."

"Just standing, reading a book," said Fagin dramatically. "Right?"

"Hey, what're you getting at, Fagin?" asked the Dodger.

But Fagin was enjoying himself too much to be hurried.

"Not riding in his carriage. Right?" he said. "Just out for a stroll?"

The Dodger studied Fagin thoughtfully. Then slowly his eyes began to sparkle and his mouth to grin.

"That's right!" he yelped. "So he weren't far from home! And Mutton Lane's near Bloomsbury. So that's where he lives. The gent lives in Bloomsbury! Is that it, Fagin?"

Fagin pinched the Dodger's cheeks gleefully. It made him proud to have his pet come up with the right answer. And it gave him special delight to show up Bill Sikes, who was still staring without comprehension.

"You're a clever boy, Dodger," said Fagin affectionately. "A credit to the establishment."

Slowly the other boys caught on, too. They clapped and stamped their feet as Fagin, in his long, loose robe, took the Dodger by the hands and began dancing wildly around the table. Bill looked on stupidly, muttering to himself, trying to figure it all out. Then, slowly, a glimmer of comprehension showed in his eyes. He stood up and pulled Fagin and the Dodger apart.

101

"Hey, listen!" he said. "I bet the old guy lives in Bloomsbury. I bet we could find him in Bloomsbury."

"Three cheers," said Fagin. "Give Bill enough time, and he'll always come up with the answer."

Bill Sikes would have jumped Fagin for this insult, but the old man was already busy. Running around the room like a sheepdog, he was herding the boys out of the door.

"Now listen, all of you," he said. "Dodger, Charlie, keep your eyes skinned. Spread yourselves about and when you find Oliver come back here at once and let me know where he is. And hurry!" he called from the bridge. "There'll be a penny for the first one to find Oliver."

Reentering the loft, Fagin went quickly to Nancy, who had been staring out the window since Bill's rebuff. The old man tried to comfort her, telling her that Bill would be fine again as soon as Oliver was back. But Nancy said nothing. Finally Fagin gave up. Scratching his beard worriedly, he went to join Bill by the fire.

CHAPTER 11

The next morning the sun shone brightly again. And Blooms-bury Square, far from Fagin's den, fairly glistened. The square was an elegant green park, rich with trees and sweet-scented flowers. Around it ran a wide, clean cobblestone street which was lined with fine houses—formal, white, and expensive-look-ing. As the sun warmed the square, birds in the green trees chirped cheerfully. And slowly from the dingy back alleys of poorer London, the shabby street vendors began to emerge, blending their plaintive songs with the cheerful ones of the birds, and gently rousing the wealthy ladies and gentlemen of Bloomsbury Square.

The first vendor to arrive was a pretty flower girl, about Bet's age.

"Who will buy my sweet red roses?" she piped.

Reaching into her flat basket, she waved several crimson buds toward the sparkling windows. "Two blooms for a penny," she sang.

More and more vendors began to appear. A milkmaid with two buckets hanging from a yoke across her shoulders, and a strawberry vendor—a plump jolly woman with cheeks to match her wares. Their cries mingled musically with the song of the flower girl.

Then came the onion man, the costermongers, errand boys, and the knife grinder. And slowly the houses, too, seemed to wake to the day, as maids and stewards hurried to receive provisions, barter over prices, sweep mats, or shake mops out of windows.

At last the finely clad ladies and gentlemen of the square were lured out to take the air, swinging canes and twirling parasols to protect white skin from the bright sun.

And someone else was stirred from sleep by the sounds of the morning. In one of the fine houses facing the square, Oliver Twist awoke to find himself in a soft, striped nightgown, tucked cozily in a tremendous, soft bed. Never before had he slept in a real bed and he found the luxurious comfort of clean white sheets and feather quilts so astonishing that, for a moment, he could not remember where he was. Even his hair was soft and clean! Then, looking about the carpeted room, he remembered coming in a horse-drawn carriage with Mr. Brownlow, whose kindly stout housekeeper, Mrs. Bedwin, had fed and bathed him and tucked him into bed.

Across the room lace curtains drifted before an open French

door. Hearing the lovely cries of the vendors, Oliver climbed out of bed and rushed out onto the balcony. By this time the early risers had been joined by others. On the green, school children paused to romp by a clear pond and prim nurses in white stockings paraded fancy baby carriages. To Oliver it all seemed a wonderful dream and, with the music of the vendors in his ears and the warm sun on his face, he, too, wanted to sing.

"Who will buy?" cried the vendors over their strawberries and flowers and fish. And Oliver thought to himself that never in his life would he wish for anything as fine as this glorious, beautiful, wonderful morning. But could it possibly last?

Oliver did not know it, but already something not so beautiful and pleasant was waiting for him. Lurking in the shadows of a large tree on the green and peering wickedly up at the balcony where Oliver stood was Bill Sikes.

Unaware of Bill's presence, Oliver would have gone on dreaming blissfully all morning had not Mrs. Bedwin broken good-naturedly into his reverie.

"Oliver!" she scolded. "What are you doing out there? You'll catch your death of cold." She put her arms around Oliver and tickled him in the ribs.

"Oh, Mrs. Bedwin," he giggled. "It's such a beautiful morning!"

"Well, maybe it is," said the kindly housekeeper. "But you come in here just the same."

Oliver followed her inside as she went on chattering about not catching fevers, and growing up to be a big strong boy. She explained that Dr. Grimwig, a special friend of Mr. Brownlow's, was downstairs waiting to meet Oliver. He was to dress in a hurry and come down for breakfast with the two men.

"May I wear my new clothes?" asked Oliver.

108

"Well you certainly can't wear the old ones," said Mrs. Bedwin with disgust. "They've all gone into the furnace. Now hurry," she said as she closed the door. "They're waiting for you!"

At breakfast Oliver sat quietly, comparing Dr. Grimwig with his name. The "wig" part did not exactly suit him. He had considerable hair on his head, and it was obviously his own. But Oliver though the "grim" part of Dr. Grimwig's name was very appropriate. Stout and red-faced, the doctor was a gruff, angry sort of man. Nothing suited him and he constantly interrupted his friend with phrases such as "Yes, but——" and "I said all along that it wouldn't work." Somewhat fearful of the doctor's grumbling, Oliver ate breakfast in respectful silence.

"Well, Oliver," said Mr. Brownlow, at last. "Have you enjoyed your breakfast?"

"Oh, yes indeed, sir!" said Oliver. "Thank you very much."

Mr. Brownlow smiled affectionately and directed Oliver to stand before his friend. After all that the boy had been through, kind Mr. Brownlow wanted him checked over by the doctor.

Oliver's speculations about Dr. Grimwig proved correct. A confirmed pessimist, he was determined to find something wrong with Oliver.

"He looks bright enough," said the doctor. "But I expect he's not sleeping well at all. Not sleeping are you, boy?" he said to Oliver.

"Oh yes, sir," said Oliver cheerfully. "I slept splendidly!"

The doctor seemed almost disappointed. "Ah," he said, brightening. "But you have bad dreams, don't you? Dreadful nightmares, eh, boy?"

"No, sir," said Oliver. "I don't dream at all."

"Come now, Grimwig," said Mr. Brownlow good-naturedly. "Stop looking for the worst. The boy feels fine."

There was a knock at the door and Mrs. Bedwin entered. She was about to go shopping and wondered if Oliver would like to go along. Seeing the boy's enthusiasm, Mr. Brownlow agreed.

Oliver excused himself and skipped toward the door. There he hesitated a moment, looking back anxiously at Mr. Brownlow.

"But, sir?" he said. "You won't send me away yet, will you?"

Mr. Brownlow opened his mouth to protest, but Oliver went on.

"I'd like to stay and be your servant, sir," he said. "May I, sir?"

"Well, well," chuckled Mr. Brownlow. "We'll see about that later."

Oliver grinned with delight at the small bit of encouragement.

"Yes, *sir!*" he said. "Thank you!"

When Oliver had gone, Mr. Brownlow spoke seriously to his friend about the boy.

"Grimwig," he said finally, "the lad has won my heart completely. I've more than half a mind to give him a real home. Now, what would you say to that?"

Dr. Grimwig took a pinch of snuff from a silver snuffbox. He sniffed it deeply and sneezed violently.

"I know only two sorts of boys," he said grimly. "Mealy boys and beefy boys."

"And Oliver?"

"Mealy," said the doctor. "Can't trust mealy boys. You mark my words, he'll repay your kindness by deceiving you. Maybe he didn't steal your wallet the other day. But he probably would have if someone else hadn't beaten him to it. He's mealy and he's an orphan. You know nothing about him."

Mr. Brownlow frowned thoughtfully and then tried to share something of what was in his heart with his friend. He admitted that he knew nothing of Oliver, yet there was something strange between them.

"There's something about him that reminds me of—well, I can't explain it," he said. "But, Grimwig, I almost feel as if I've *seen* him somewhere—somewhere a long time ago."

"Nonsense!" exploded Dr. Grimwig. "Stuff and nonsense! You're so sentimental and conscience-stricken about getting the boy into trouble that you're imagining things!"

"I suppose so," sighed Mr. Brownlow. "But all the same I can't help thinking . . ."

CHAPTER 12

It did not take Oliver long to feel at home at Mr. Brownlow's house. Past troubles seemed far behind and several nights later, as he was falling peacefully asleep in his cozy bed, Oliver could not have imagined that his old friends were thinking of him. Nevertheless, in a certain quarter of London, a ragged few were worrying away the night because of Oliver Twist.

Sprawled about the floor and rafters of Fagin's loft, the Artful Dodger, Charlie Bates, and the other pickpockets had no thoughts of sleep. In a chair by the fire the terrible Bill Sikes pounded a fist into his palm and cursed under his breath. Completely ignored, Nancy sat again by the window, her face drawn with conflict and worry. Fagin alone prowled about the room, plucking nervously at his beard.

The tension was ominous and the cause of it all was the continued absence of Oliver. After days of watching the Brownlow house, Bill had still been unable to catch Oliver alone. Yet there could be no peace in Fagin's loft until Oliver was back. Any minute, they were certain, the town constables would be at the door ready to lock up the whole establishment on the basis of information given to them by Oliver. Had Oliver known all this he would have gladly put his friends' minds at ease. As far as he was concerned, they had all been kind to him and it had not entered his mind to cause them any trouble.

The sagging floor of the loft creaked irritatingly as Fagin paced—now toward the door, now back to the fireplace. Suddenly Bill Sikes could stand it no longer. An unmeditative man to begin with, he now rose angrily to his feet, causing the boys to sit up and startling Fagin and Nancy to attention.

"You got to do something!" he roared. "It's been three days since I seen the kid at that house and you haven't done nothing! And quit pacing around like that, you mangy old scarecrow," he said to Fagin. "You get on my nerves! Why don't you *do* something?"

Bill ranted on, the light of the flames dancing wildly across his face. He was sure that Oliver had blabbed his head off already and they'd all be in the gallows soon. If Fagin was so smart why hadn't he done something? In Bill Sikes, anger bred more anger. He grabbed the old man by the throat.

"If you don't get that blasted kid back tomorrow, I'll kill you," he raged.

Suddenly Nancy spoke, her voice soft and soothing.

114

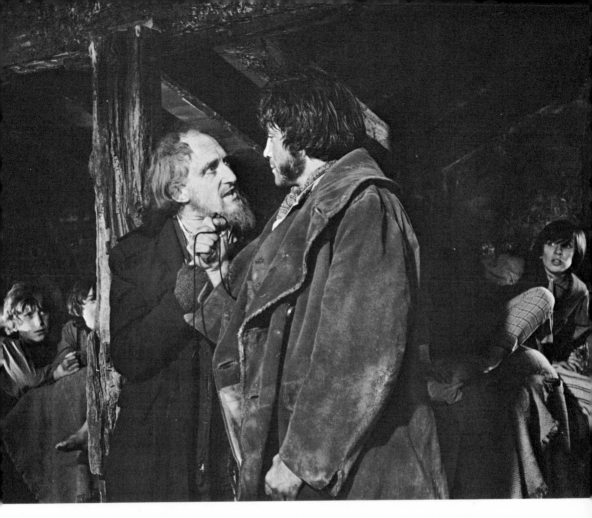

"Bill," she said. "It isn't that easy. You know he never comes out of that house alone."

"And you just shut up," shouted Bill. "Don't you talk back to me. I've had just about enough out of you, too."

He turned back to Fagin, demanding to know who was going to fetch Oliver. He did not see the sudden cold look on Nancy's face. Nobody did.

Instead, all eyes were on Fagin as he cast his eye about the room for the right person to get Oliver. It was no good sending Bill. The constables might already be looking for him. Besides, Bill would create too much of a scene. The Dodger volunteered, but he had fallen from grace in Fagin's eyes and was no longer considered trustworthy.

"You shut your trap, Dodger," snarled Fagin. "You've made us enough trouble already, letting Oliver get caught."

His eyes fell thoughtfully on Nancy, who was staring out the window again, her back toward the room. Perhaps she was worried for Oliver, perhaps for herself. But whichever it was, Fagin could see that she, too, had had just about enough. Still, who else was there?

"Nancy, my dear," he said sweetly, "how would *you* like to fetch back our dear little Oliver?"

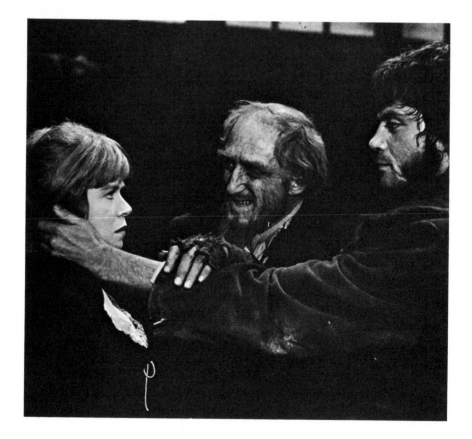

Without turning around Nancy spoke coldly. "Uh-uh," she said, "it's no good trying it on me."

Bill stomped across the room and, taking Nancy by the chin, spun her around. "And just what do you mean by that remark?" he said menacingly.

For the first time, Nancy spoke defiantly to Bill. Jerking herself free of his grasp, she rose to her feet and glared at him. "I mean just what I say," she snapped. "I'm not going. Why can't you leave the boy alone? He won't do you no harm. Leave him alone—let him have the chance of a decent life."

For a second Bill looked at her, stunned and outraged at her defiance. Then, unable to put his anger into words, he grabbed her by the shoulders and flung her into a chair.

"She'll go, Fagin," he said.

"No, she *won't,* Fagin," said Nancy firmly.

"Yes, she will," snarled Bill. As he spoke he raised his arm deliberately and struck her viciously across the face, knocking her to the floor. Then, without looking back, he turned and strode toward the door. Bullseye crept out from under the table and followed.

"She'll go," said Bill as he closed the door. "She'll go if I have to drag her there myself."

All this time Fagin had been darting uncertainly about the loft, wanting to intercede on Nancy's behalf but shrinking from violence. Now he hurried to Nancy and tried nervously to help her to her feet.

Pushing Fagin aside, Nancy stood up painfully and went slowly after Bill. From the rooftop bridge she watched sadly as Bill and Bullseye made their way over the canal bridge below. Viewed from such a distance, the bully appeared strangely unprotected and forlorn.

"He *does* need me," Nancy whispered. "In spite of the way he treats me, I know he needs me."

She began to hurry, rushing across the bridge and down the stairs.

"No matter what happens," she said softly, "it's him I got to stick by."

CHAPTER 13

The next afternoon at Mr. Brownlow's house a uniformed maid was carrying a silver tray with afternoon tea for Mr. Brownlow and Dr. Grimwig. The doorbell jangled, and she was just about to put down the tray and answer the door when Oliver came bounding down the curved staircase.

"I'll get it, Rose," he said cheerfully. "You go ahead with the tea."

He skipped across the carpeted hall and opened the study door. "Thanks, love," said the maid as she went through with the tray.

Oliver walked grandly to the front door and opened it.

"Books from Mr. Jessop for Mr. Brownlow," said an errand boy.

"Thank you!" said Oliver. He took the books from the boy, then closing the door quietly he hurried to the study. It was a small, cozy room furnished with comfortable leather chairs and filled with book-laden shelves that testified to Mr. Brownlow's love of literature. Of all the rooms in the house the study was Oliver's favorite. Mr. Brownlow was already teaching him to read and Oliver could scarcely wait until he could read for himself some of the fine volumes he saw in the study.

When Oliver entered Mrs. Bedwin was just pouring tea for the two gentlemen, who were concentrating on a game of chess. Mr. Brownlow looked up at Oliver and smiled. Dr. Grimwig frowned.

"Your move, Brownlow!" he said, irritated by the interruption.

"If you please, sir," said Oliver to Mr. Brownlow. "These books just came for you."

"Ah, good!" said Mr. Brownlow. He stood up from the chess table. "And there are some to go back," he said.

"The boy's gone, sir," said Oliver. "But let me take them back for you. I know where the shop is and I'll be very quick. Please, sir, may I take them?"

Oliver waited, fidgeting with excitement. This was his chance to prove to Mr. Brownlow that he could be a useful and responsible servant. The kind man seemed doubtful for a moment. Then with a look of resolution he nodded.

"All right," he said. "You shall go! Mrs. Bedwin, the books are by my bed."

Mrs. Bedwin went off to get the books and Dr. Grimwig spoke

up testily. "Come along, Brownlow!" he said. "It's your move, man!"

Ignoring the doctor, Mr. Brownlow took out his wallet and handed Oliver a five-pound note. He explained that Oliver should deliver the books to Mr. Jessop personally.

"And tell him you've also come to pay the four pounds ten I owe him for that other book. This is a five-pound note," he said, "so there will be ten shillings change. Do you understand?"

"Yes, sir!" said Oliver. "I'll be back in ten minutes."

He turned to go, but his eye fell on a small oil painting that he

had not noticed before. It was hanging on the wall by the door—a portrait of a young woman about Nancy's age and something about it caught his eye. For a moment he stared at it, fascinated.

Mr. Brownlow watched Oliver with interest. He walked over and put his arm around the boy.

"What is it, Oliver?" he asked gently. "Are you fond of pictures?"

"I really don't know, sir," said Oliver. "I've only seen a few of them, but—" he stared at the picture intently. "She's a very pretty lady, isn't she, sir?"

Mr. Brownlow looked back and forth between Oliver and the picture.

"There's a lady I dream about sometimes . . ." Oliver said slowly. Then, suddenly embarrassed by Mr. Brownlow's intense interest, he remembered his errand.

"I'm sorry, sir," he said brightly. "I'll be going with the books now."

For a moment after Oliver had closed the study door Mr. Brownlow continued to look at the portrait. Dr. Grimwig finally broke the silence.

"Hmph!" he said. "You don't expect him to come back, do you?"

"Don't you?" asked Mr. Brownlow with surprise.

"With a new suit of clothes on his back, a set of valuable books under his arm and a five-pound note in his pocket?" laughed the doctor. "I should say not! My dear Brownlow, if he ever returns to this house I'll eat my head *with* my hat on it!"

Suddenly Mr. Brownlow swung around.

"No, you're wrong," he said. "Grimwig, you're quite wrong. Just look at that portrait!"

Mr. Brownlow led his friend to the portrait on the wall.

122

"Don't you see the likeness? The likeness between Oliver and this portrait?" he said.

"Bless my soul, man!" cried Dr. Grimwig. "Have you taken leave of your senses?" He raised his arms in a gesture of helplessness. Then, putting a hand on Mr. Brownlow's arm, he began to reason with him almost patiently.

"They are both young," he said. "They are both innocent. But that's all there is to it—a mere coincidence. Come now, man—you're entirely overwrought!"

It was obvious that no amount of talking would convince the

123

doctor that there was any special resemblance between the portrait and Oliver Twist. Mr. Brownlow sat down at his desk and took out a sheet of writing paper. Though he continued to talk aloud, he was clearly oblivious of his friend's presence.

"No," he muttered. "It's more than coincidence. There's some sort of a mystery here and I mean to solve it. I intend to find out who the boy is. All right, he says he was born in a workhouse —at Dunstable, he thinks. Very well then, I shall write to the workhouse this minute."

Dr. Grimwig watched Mr. Brownlow as he began to write furiously. Then, resigning himself to the fact that the chess game was over, he shrugged his shoulders and went home.

CHAPTER 14

Mrs. Bedwin handed Oliver the books, kissed him lightly on the cheek, and sent him on his way. So happy was the boy with his new responsibility that he did not notice Nancy and Bill lurking under the tree on the green. Nor did he see Bill signal Nancy to follow Oliver, pushing her roughly when she hung back.

The books were bound with a leather strap and Oliver swung them gaily as he sped toward the bookshop, which had brought him first such terror and later such good fortune. At the corner he smiled at the pretty flower girl who had sung so sweetly on his first morning in Bloomsbury. Impulsively the girl chucked

125

him under the chin with one hand and stuck a rose in his button-hole with the other.

Oliver headed down a side street, unaware that he was being followed. At the entrance to an alley, a good-sized crowd had gathered. From somewhere in the middle of the crowd a nasal voice cried, "Only a penny a bottle! A spoonful taken night and morning, ladies and gents, will cure your bunions and boils like magic!"

Standing on tiptoe, and craning his neck, Oliver could just see the speaker—a vendor of patent medicines, who was doing a good job of proclaiming his wares.

Oliver lingered with the crowd. During his short time in London he had seen numerous vendors and listened to the fantastic claims they made about their wares. But never had he heard one use so many or such big words as this man did without even seeming to stop for breath.

The vendor waved a dark-looking bottle in the air.

"Guaranteed to cure all the ailments which the flesh is heir to," he cried.

A woman abounding in both flesh and apparent good health stepped forward to purchase a bottle. The crowd tittered.

"Guaranteed to relieve the fever, stop the toothache, and re-move spots from the sarcophagus," continued the vendor, "this remarkable fluid will also promote the growth of luxuriant hair upon the head, improve the appetite, and increase the flow of blood through veins and arteries."

In spite of the general amusement on the part of the spec-tators, more and more people stepped forward to invest in the vendor's magic potion. Oliver was so entranced that he did not see Nancy and Bill with Bullseye on a leash as they joined the crowd not far from the spot where he was standing. Bill gave

Nancy an angry shove and she moved around and stood behind the unsuspecting Oliver.

"Step right up, ladies, and gents," the vendor coaxed.

Suddenly Oliver was being jerked out of the crowd. He looked up to find Nancy gripping his arms painfully, her face full of remorse.

"What is it?" cried Oliver. "Nancy, let me go!"

"You've got to come with me," said Nancy.

Oliver struggled desperately as Nancy pulled him around the edge of the crowd toward the spot where Bill was standing.

"Let me go, please!" he pleaded loudly. "I won't come. I won't!"

A man from the crowd turned to intervene. Automatically he assumed that Oliver was making trouble for Nancy.

"What's the matter, ma'am?" he asked.

Dramatically Nancy flung her arms around Oliver in a sudden display of affection.

"I've found him at last," she cried. "Oh, thank heavens. I've found my dear little brother."

More and more people turned their backs on the vendor to watch what was going on in the street. In spite of Oliver's loud protests, Nancy continued with her story. The boy was her dear little brother, she said. He had run away from home—nearly two weeks ago—and had joined a lot of thieves and bad characters. He had almost broken his poor mother's heart. And Nancy was putting on a convincing display of grief, too.

"It's not true!" Oliver cried. "You know I haven't a mother. Please! Please, let me go, Nancy!"

But Nancy had already won the heart of the crowd—especially of the women.

"Go home, you little brute!" cried one.

127

"The ungrateful wretch!" said another.

"Why, what the devil is this?" said Bill, pushing through the crowd. He picked Oliver up by the back of his collar, holding him at arm's length so that he could only kick the air futilely.

"You young dog!" he said. "You come right home to your poor mother. At once, do you hear?"

Oliver knew better than to try to plead with Bill Sikes. So he turned instead to the crowd for mercy, telling them that he didn't belong to Bill and Nancy, and begging for their help.

But if Oliver had had any supporters in the crowd, he lost them in the next second. Bill grabbed Mr. Brownlow's books and held them up before the onlookers.

"Stealing again, eh?" he said. "Take that, you little wretch!"

He cuffed Oliver across the face.

"That's it!" cried a man. "That's what he needs."

"Give him a good hiding," said another.

With Bullseye snapping at his heels and Nancy and Bill on either side of him, Oliver was dragged helplessly away.

CHAPTER 15

The walk across town was long and silent. Bill, as sullen as ever, took no notice of Nancy's quiet, troubled mood. And Oliver knew better than to say anything. He did not struggle, but walked along obediently between his two captors, noticing for the first time how dreary and filthy the poorer section of London was. With Mr. Brownlow's fine house for comparison, Oliver found it hard to believe that the stinking, tumbledown tenements were actually the homes of human beings. In spite of his own frightening predicament, he felt sorry for the people who had to live there.

It was dark as the three crossed the plank bridge over the garbage-filled canal and started up the stairs toward Fagin's loft. From the rooftop bridge, Fagin called anxiously down to them, "Who's there? Who is it?"

"It ain't the beak, if that's what you're worrying about," said Bill. "We've brought the brat."

He dragged Oliver up the stairs and shoved him across the bridge to Fagin, who pulled him inside.

"Ah ha!" said Fagin. "So you've come back to your dear old friends at last, my dear."

He pushed Oliver forward and sent him stumbling across the room into the eager arms of the Dodger and the other boys.

Never had Oliver felt less at home or more out of place. Without so much as a single word of welcome, the boys crowded around Oliver, pulling off his fancy clothes and jeering at him.

"Would you look at his togs?" said the Dodger.

"And see the pretty posy in his buttonhole," teased another.

"Yeah, Oliver's real cute, ain't he?" taunted Charlie Bates. "Quite the little gent, ain't you Oliver?"

Oliver stood stock-still as, one by one, his new possessions were torn from him. He clung fiercely to the bundle of books, praying that these would not be taken from him. But even that was too much to hope.

"Hey, look at that!" cried Charlie. "He's even got books!"

Charlie grabbed the books and sprang up onto a rafter. From a pocket he produced a pair of glassless spectacles through which he began peering at the books.

"I'm a real scholar, I am!" he said grandly.

The boys howled with laughter.

All this time the Dodger was going systematically through Oliver's pockets. Oliver said nothing. He was speechless with

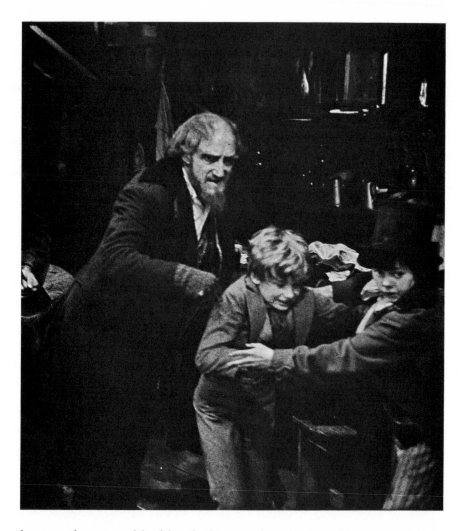

hurt and rage at his friends for turning against him. Nothing in his harsh life had prepared him for such a betrayal.

Suddenly the Dodger let out a whoop and pulled out Mr. Brownlow's five-pound note. Backing defensively from the rest of the group, he held up the note for all to see.

"Blimey!" he cried. "Look at this, would you?"

Fagin's long fingers actually seemed to grow longer as he

reached out greedily for the money. But Bill Sikes, too, was ready to contest ownership with the Dodger. Poor Dodger was the first to lose out as Fagin and Bill snatched and grabbed the money from each other.

"If you don't hand it over," Bill threatened, "I'll take the boy back again."

"No, my dear," said Fagin. "It's mine. You can have the books."

The two argued fiercely for the note. With financial gain at stake Fagin seemed almost brave—even in the face of Bill Sikes.

At last it was too much for Oliver to bear. They could do what they liked with him, but the money and the books belonged to Mr. Brownlow. Mr. Brownlow had trusted him. To look like a thief in that kind man's eyes was the worst thing that could happen. He rushed across the room and flung himself on Bill, hitting him with all his might and struggling mightily to regain the five-pound note.

"You can't," he shrieked. "You can't have the money *or* the books. They belong to Mr. Brownlow!"

Again Bill dangled Oliver in the air with one hand, holding the money a short tantalizing distance away.

"Please, please!" pleaded Oliver as he struggled to get free. "Please send them back. He'll think I stole them!"

"Well that's fine, ain't it?" said Bill with a grin. "He'll reckon you're a thief and then he won't bother about you at all any more, will he?"

Oliver kicked the big man hard on the shin. The crack could be heard around the room, and the other boys stood in stunned silence, waiting to see what the terrible man would do. The fun was over.

Bill threw Oliver over a table and began unclasping his belt. "Kick me, would you?" he hissed.

Oliver crouched over the tabletop, shaking with fear and sobbing quietly. Bill raised his heavy, studded belt, but suddenly from behind there came a hand to hold him back.

Since entering Fagin's loft, Nancy had remained quiet and unobserved. Amid the clowning and arguing, no one had noticed her as she looked first at Bill, then at Oliver, and then again at Bill. Now, as she grabbed Bill's arm, it was evident to all that she was fairly shaking with mixed emotions. She loved Bill Sikes, everyone knew that. But she could not stand by and watch him beat a helpless child.

"No!" she said as she took Bill's arm. "I won't let you hurt the boy."

"A fine one you are to stick up for the kid," said Bill. "You're in this just as deep as the rest of us, you know."

Nancy was clearly stung by the truth and cruelty of his words. But she could not be deterred from defending Oliver.

"That's right," she said. "And I wish I'd been struck dead before having any part in it." Then, as Fagin ventured forward to make peace, Nancy suddenly turned on him.

"And you!" she said. "I thieved for you when I was half his age and I've done your dirty work for you ever since. But I'm sick to death of you and your selfishness. I'm not going to stand here and watch this boy beaten to death for no reason."

Nobody moved. This was not the Nancy they all knew—faithful to Bill Sikes, fun-loving, carefree. To defy Bill under any circumstances was unheard of, much less in front of Fagin and the boys! It was so astounding that for a long moment nobody moved. Even Bill was momentarily silent. Then, slowly lowering his arm, he took Nancy by the wrist and swaggered toward the door. But Oliver sensed that there was something unsure about the big man now.

Fagin had no trouble getting the boys to bed that night. What had started out as fun had turned into something frightening and sad. They didn't like Nancy to be unhappy. And Nancy had stung their consciences. They had only meant to poke fun at Oliver, but they knew they had gone too far. Seeing Nancy angry, and Bill Sikes quiet turned their world upside-down. The game of clowning and picking pockets was suddenly real and frightening. Something bad was going to come of it for sure.

Once again, Oliver was put to bed by the fire. A couple of

135

boys tiptoed by him and, when no one was looking whispered, "Sorry, old man . . . didn't mean no harm . . . glad to see you back, mate." But their words brought little comfort to Oliver. As on his first night in Fagin's establishment, he lay awake unable to sleep.

Just as before he watched Fagin make his nightly rounds, muttering to himself like a madman and counting his secret treasures. But this time Oliver noticed that Fagin, too, was troubled and upset. As the old man bent for the box that was hidden beneath the floor by the fire, Oliver could hear him arguing with himself.

"It's distressing," he muttered. "I don't like this business with little Oliver at all. I'm no saint—I'm a villain, in fact—but I never meant for no one to get hurt. Maybe I should give up this line of work . . . send all the lads to school. Ah, but then who'd be left to take care of me in my old age?"

For some time the old miser went on reviewing the situation. He was genuinely worried about Oliver and the boys, but he was also concerned about his old age.

"On the one hand," he mused, "I could get a job and support them all . . . but on the other hand I don't like work. . . . A wife? A wife! In the first place I'll get me a wife to cook and sew for me and the boys . . . and in the second place, with my luck, she'll nag me to death!"

Every time poor Fagin came up with a new alternative he found a hitch in it and had to reconsider. Every time he thought he had a new solution he found himself confronted by a new conflict of interest.

"No," he said finally, "I'm a villain and a villain I'll stay. But . . ." he paused, frowning. "There's going to be trouble. Someone's going to get hurt. I think I'll have to think it out again."

If he had not been in such a predicament himself, Oliver would have laughed outright at the crazy old skinflint. And even with his own troubles to worry about, he could not help feeling sorry for Fagin. Maybe he was greedy, but he was not mean. And Oliver had to admit that life with Fagin was much better than life in the workhouse. He turned over in his sacking bed and tried to sleep, but his thoughts turned once more to Bill. Sooner or later Bill would be back and he was not likely to forget what had happened.

More than anything, Oliver longed to be back with Mr. Brownlow. But probably Mr. Brownlow wouldn't have him even if Oliver could find a way to escape. If only he could manage to get the books and money back to Mr. Brownlow. . . .

CHAPTER 16

Days went by and Oliver still had not found a way to get Mr. Brownlow's books and money back to him. Fagin treated him well enough and the boys were as friendly to him as ever. But Oliver was kept close to home and more or less under guard. The boys went off pocket-picking each day as usual, but Oliver was not invited nor did he wish to go along. He sat about in the loft, toasting sausages over the fire for Fagin when he was told to and watching the old man scurry about the den—chattering to himself and hiding things like a worried squirrel. There was one thing for which Oliver was grateful and that was that Bill Sikes had not returned.

Then, one night when the boys were rather late in returning home, the door opened and in walked Bill Sikes.

"Why, Bill, my dear!" said Fagin with his best charm. "What brings you here at this time? I thought you'd be out on that little job we was talking about."

"I'm just going," snarled Bill. "But I need a boy."

"They're all out," said Fagin. "Nobody's home but me and dear little Oliver—and I don't think you'd be needing him now, would you?"

"I'll have to take him," Bill said. "I need a brat to get through the window and open the door for me."

"But you can't take Oliver," said Fagin. "You know he wouldn't be any use to you. Besides, maybe they've got the beaks out looking for him."

Oliver held his breath.

"Do you want the job done, or don't you?" challenged Bill.

For a moment Fagin seemed uncertain. He looked back and forth at Oliver and Bill, reviewing the situation.

"All right," he said at last. "All right, then, take him."

"Greedy old man," sneered Bill. "I knew you'd see it that way."

Oliver cowered in the chimney kitchen, where he had been sweeping. But there was no escaping Bill Sikes, who soon had a firm grip on Oliver's shoulder.

Before going out on the job, Bill had to stop at home to pick up his tools. Nancy watched in dumfounded alarm as Bill led Oliver, pale and trembling, through the doorway. Even though it was Nancy who had captured him, Oliver was relieved to see her. With all his heart he hoped she would stop Bill from taking him.

Without a word of greeting, Bill strode across the room and began pulling out chests of tools from under the narrow bed. He picked up a small crowbar and stuck it in his belt.

"What's going on?" said Nancy at last. "Why have you brought the boy here?"

"He's coming on the job," said Bill.

Nancy was incredulous and frightened. She could not see what possible use Oliver could be to Bill and, knowing how Bill felt about him, she was sure that something would happen to Oliver.

"But why?" she exclaimed. "Why *him?*"

Bill slammed down the lid of his tool box and glared at Nancy. As usual he was furious with her for questioning him. "It's none of your business," he said, "but I need a little one, that's why. And there wasn't anyone else."

He opened a drawer and took out a heavy pistol. He weighed

it momentarily in his hand. Then, after checking to make sure it was loaded, he suddenly pressed the barrel against Oliver's cheek.

"You know what happens if you open your mouth now, don't you?" he said.

Oliver nodded. Then as Bill turned to pick up a lantern,

Oliver looked pitifully to Nancy for help.

"Must I go?" he whispered.

Frantically Nancy pleaded with Bill. "You can't do this to him, Bill," she said. "He won't be any good to you. He's not like the others. He's scared to death."

But Bill was already halfway out the door with Oliver.

"Just be at the Three Cripples around eleven," he said.

Crouching behind a wealthy house, Oliver listened numbly as Bill explained what he was to do. He was to crawl through a small window that led to a downstairs pantry. Once inside Bill would give him a lantern. He was to take the lantern, and tip-toe through the pantry and up some stairs. At the top of the stairs he would find himself in the front hall. He was to open the front door and let Bill in. The rest of the robbery would be up to Bill. The bully waggled his pistol in front of Oliver's face.

"And mind you, not a peep," he threatened. "One peep out of you and you're dead."

"Please, Mr. Sikes," Oliver pleaded. "Please don't make me."

"What did I tell you," the big man hissed.

Oliver nodded, his teeth chattering from fear and cold. He turned and slipped through the small window that Bill held open and then reached up for the lantern. Under the circumstances the pantry was a frightening place to be. The light from the lantern was poor and Oliver gasped as something feathery brushed his cheek. It was a dead partridge hanging limply by its feet from the ceiling. Back and forth it swung in the lamp light, its lifeless eyes gleaming accusingly at Oliver.

The stairs were few, but each one creaked treacherously. With every step he took, Oliver was sure that one of the servants asleep upstairs would wake up. But at long last he found himself in the front hall. There the floor was well carpeted, so it was easier to walk quietly. But suddenly there was a loud squeak at the front door. Oliver spun around, his eyes wild with terror. Peering through the mail slot in the door, were two eyes. Someone was watching him.

"Hurry," said a voice in a hoarse whisper. "Get on with it!"

It was Bill Sikes waiting on the front step for Oliver to open the door.

Oliver tiptoed across the carpet and reached up to release the latch. But he was too small. The bolt was quite beyond his reach. He looked about the hallway in panic. Then he spotted a chair, which he fetched and placed in front of the door. By climbing onto the chair and standing on tiptoe he could just reach the bolt. But the bolt was tight. Though Oliver strained to move it, it refused to budge. He tried again, leaning into it with all his might. Suddenly, it gave way. For one terrible second Oliver swayed precariously. Then, unable to regain his balance, he slipped off the chair, knocking it over with a loud crash.

Immediately there came the sound of a man's voice from upstairs. Feet rushed about overhead as the servants of the house quickly woke to protect the house.

"What's that," someone cried. "Toby! John! Wake up! There's someone downstairs."

Somewhere in the house two dogs began barking excitedly.

The front door flew open and Bill grabbed Oliver.

"Hurry up!" he whispered. "Come on!"

Ducking around the house, the two headed for the wall over which they had entered the back yard. At the back of the house a window flew open and a pistol shot rang out as Bill flung Oliver over the wall and then came scrambling over behind him.

145

As Oliver hit the ground he felt a tremendous pain in his ankle.

"Run, brat," hissed Bill. "Run or I'll leave you here and let them shoot you!"

"I can't," Oliver whimpered. "My ankle!"

Then he was riding on Bill Sikes's shoulder as the big man ran and ran into the dark alleys of London. Once again cries of "Stop, thief!" fell on Oliver's ears and he realized with horror that he, too, was being chased. And this time he was guilty. Though nothing had been stolen he, Oliver Twist, had entered someone's home without permission. But slowly the angry shouts, the pistol shots, and the barking faded in the distance. Oliver could hear only the panting and cursing of Bill Sikes.

CHAPTER 17

On the night that Oliver was with Bill Sikes, Mr. Brownlow received a series of unexpected visitors. The first to present themselves at the door in Bloomsbury Square were Oliver's old guardians, Mr. Bumble and the Widow Corney. Since Oliver's departure from the workhouse the two had married. But marriage had not changed them a bit. They alternately flirted and quarreled with each other and both were as self-seeking as ever.

With a ridiculously pompous manner, Mr. Bumble tried to speak eloquently with Mr. Brownlow in the library.

"And so, you see, sir," he said, "the instant I received your communication regarding dear little Oliver I decided we must take the first coach to London."

"*I* decided," interrupted Widow Corney. Wedlock had not taught either of them the advantages of sharing and in the present situation each wanted the credit and, hopefully, the reward to himself.

"Well, er, yes," admitted Mr. Bumble with disappointment. "My dear wife decided."

Not at all deceived by the airs and false grandeur of his two guests, Mr. Brownlow was anxious to hear what they had to say.

"It was good of you both to come," he said, trying to be patient. "Now just what is it that you have to tell me?"

Rolling his head about like an embarrassed schoolboy, Mr.

Bumble squeezed two chubby fingers into the watch pocket of his overstuffed vest. Hemming and hawing grandly, he produced the locket and chain which the Widow Corney had taken from Oliver's mother on the night that Oliver was born.

"This little trinket, sir," he said, "was given by the boy's mother to my dear wife before she passed away. Before the mother passed away that is." He giggled. "Not my dear wife as you can see."

He swung the locket about in an embarrassed way and then, still chuckling awkwardly over his joke, pressed it desperately into Mr. Brownlow's palm.

For a long moment Mr. Brownlow stared at the locket. His eyes filled with tears and he turned abruptly to pace about the room until he could contain his emotion. His two visitors shifted uncomfortably from one foot to the other.

In a sudden fury Mr. Brownlow stepped toward Widow Corney, his face full of accusation.

"You mean to tell me that the mother *gave* this locket to *you*? And you've kept it all these years?" he said sharply.

Widow Corney looked shiftily toward her husband and then stared fiercely at Mr. Brownlow. "Why shouldn't she have gave it to me?" she challenged. "Why shouldn't I have kept it?"

"Did it not occur to you that it might provide the answer to the boy's parentage—perhaps to his very name?"

"He had no name, sir," Mr. Bumble offered humbly. "*I* gave him his——"

Mr. Brownlow interrupted, his voice trembling with emotion.

"It was your duty to pass this evidence to a higher authority," he said to Widow Corney. "Your behavior, madam, was shameful!"

"What!" cried the woman, abruptly dropping her fine airs.

"The idea! Here we come all this way to help and all we get is——"

"No, INDEED, Madam," bellowed Mr. Brownlow. "You came here only in the hope of profiting from your own greed and dishonesty."

Mr. Bumble tried desperately to save face, but Mr. Brownlow would have none of it. Taking out his wallet, he handed his visitors a ten-pound note.

"Take that and get out!" he said, turning his back. "And consider yourselves fortunate that you don't find yourselves in the hands of the law."

Mrs. Bedwin, who had been watching the proceedings, now stepped forward to show the couple to the door. But Mr. Bumble hung back.

"I hope, sir," he said confidentially, "that this little incident won't deprive me of my office as parish beadle."

"And *my* hope, sir," shouted Mr. Brownlow, "is that it will! Now get out of my house at once!"

When Mrs. Bedwin returned from sending the Bumbles on their way, Mr. Brownlow was standing before the portrait of the young woman. He held the locket on the tips of his fingers and rubbed it gently with his thumb. Hearing Mrs. Bedwin enter, he turned, shaking his head slowly, his kind eyes full of pain. For a moment he could not speak.

"Sir," said the housekeeper. "The locket . . . I couldn't really see, but . . ."

Mr. Brownlow held out the locket for his faithful servant to examine. Her eyes grew wide with surprise.

"Yes," said Mr. Brownlow. "It belonged to my niece Emily. I gave it to her on her eighteenth birthday shortly before she disappeared. That boy is the son of my own kin. Oliver Twist is

153

my great-nephew!"

"Oh, sir!" cried Mrs. Bedwin. "How can we ever find him? We *must* find him!"

The second visitor at the Brownlow household that night was Nancy. Only a moment after Bill and Oliver had set out on the job, Nancy had slipped out into the streets and headed off resolutely in the direction of Bloomsbury.

As she stepped up to Mr. Brownlow's door and pulled the bell, she drew her shawl about her face and looked nervously up and down the street. Presently the door opened and Mrs. Bedwin peered out.

"I've come about Oliver," Nancy whispered. "But please don't tell anyone that I'm here."

"You'd better come in," said Mrs. Bedwin.

Nancy stepped reluctantly over the threshold, stopping just inside the door. She refused to go farther and pleaded with Mrs. Bedwin not to call Mr. Brownlow. She would much prefer to leave a message. But the loyal housekeeper could not be dissuaded from calling her master once Oliver's name had been mentioned.

"It's about the boy, sir," she said as Mr. Brownlow appeared at the door of his study.

Mr. Brownlow walked quickly to Nancy. He spoke cordially but with tense, impatient interest.

"You have news of him? Where is he? And, please, who are you?"

Breathlessly, Nancy said not to mind about her name, but that Oliver was in danger.

"What's happened to him?" asked Mr. Brownlow. "Who took him? And why?"

154

"Me," Nancy confessed truthfully, ". . . and . . . someone else. Lord help me, sir, I wish now I'd never been a part of it."

"But where is Oliver now?" urged Mr. Brownlow. "And who is this other person you speak of?"

"I can't tell you that," said Nancy desperately. "He'd kill me if he even knew I——"

Mr. Brownlow interrupted.

"Can you take me to the boy," he said. "Can you at least tell me where I can find him?"

"No," said Nancy. "But I'll bring him to you. Not here—at the bridge. Be at London Bridge around midnight tonight."

Unlike the Bumbles, Nancy was anxious to leave. But Mr. Brownlow detained her a moment longer, putting his hand gently on her shoulder.

"Young lady," he said, "I can't thank you enough. You cannot imagine what your coming has meant to me. But," he said kindly, "I can tell that you're frightened and in trouble. Tell me the name of this man who has Oliver. Then perhaps I can help you."

Nancy shook her head.

"No, I won't turn on him," she said. "I can't help it, but I love him."

She backed down the steps and disappeared.

CHAPTER 18

Oliver had never been in such a place as the Inn of the Three Cripples. The loud noise of singing and laughing was confusing and the smoke in the air stung his eyes. Pushed and shoved by Bill Sikes, Oliver limped through the crowd and up the stairs to the balcony where Fagin and Nancy were waiting. At the top of the stairs he sank to the floor and leaned against the railing not far from Bullseye, who was settled beneath the table. Added to the pain in his ankle and the ache in his heart, the smell of the inn made Oliver feel sick.

"Was everything all right, Bill?" asked Nancy.

"No, it wasn't all right," growled Bill. "The brat woke everybody up and we had to run for it."

As usual, Fagin was concerned first of all about profit. Had the robbery been successful? Had Bill managed to get away with anything?

"That's all you think of, ain't it?" fired Bill. "No! Of course I didn't get the swag. We were lucky enough not to get nabbed, I tell you!"

Seeing that Bill was involved with Fagin, Nancy moved slowly toward Oliver.

"You've hurt your leg," she said softly. "I saw you limping."

"No," Oliver said. "I only twisted my ankle a little when we went over the wall."

"You can walk then?" whispered Nancy.

Oliver nodded, his eyes questioning.

Nancy put a finger to her lips. "I'm taking you home," she said.

She glanced again at the table and, seeing that Bill and Fagin were still absorbed in conversation, motioned Oliver to follow her. As inconspicuously as possible, the two made their way down the stairs and through the crowd toward the door. As they slipped out into the street Nancy did not see Bill look angrily down from the balcony.

"What's *she* up to?" he said fiercely.

Throwing back his chair, he strode angrily down the stairs with Bullseye close behind him.

Outside, Nancy led Oliver across the deserted street and began walking quickly toward the river.

"But Nancy," Oliver said, "I thought you were taking me back to Fagin's. This isn't the way."

"Hush," said Nancy. "He'll kill me for this if he finds out."

She did not know that Bill was following close behind them.

As soon as the Three Cripples was out of sight, Nancy explained to Oliver that she was taking him back to Mr. Brownlow, who would be waiting for him on the London Bridge.

"But," she said, "you must never, never tell Mr. Brownlow where you've been or what you have seen. I know it's hard for you to understand, but I love Bill Sikes. You've got a chance of a better life. But I haven't. Bill's all I've got in this world and I mean to stick by him."

At the river, wide steps led up to the bridge. In the middle of the bridge, silhouetted against the sky, stood Mr. Brownlow. He did not see Oliver and Nancy as they approached.

"He thinks I'm a thief now," Oliver whispered. "What if he won't have me back?"

"He will, love," said Nancy. "Your old Nance has seen to that. Run along now."

She pushed Oliver gently toward the bridge. Slowly he limped up the steps. He stopped and turned, then rushing back he jumped into Nancy's arms, hugging her with all his might. He was happy and sad and grateful all at once.

"Oh, Nancy!" he cried. "Thank you for everything. I shall miss you terribly!"

"And I shall miss you, too, Oliver," Nancy whispered.

From a hiding place behind a bush, Bill Sikes looked on, his face grim. Now, convinced that Nancy was about to betray him, he sprang out from hiding and leaped on Nancy, sending Oliver flying through the air. As the boy watched, horrified, the big man raised a cudgel and with one blow clubbed Nancy to the ground.

"Betray me, would you?" he said hoarsely.

160

"No, Bill," Nancy whispered. "Not you—I'd never betray you."

She reached up to hug Bill, then suddenly fell limp in his arms.

From nowhere a crowd began to gather and among them, rushing from the bridge, came Mr. Brownlow. He did not see Bill grab Oliver and drag him away along the river path.

Mr. Brownlow knelt down and lifted Nancy's head into his lap.

"Who did this terrible thing?" he said. "Tell me who did this to you?"

Slowly Nancy shook her head. Then closing her eyes she whispered, "No," and died.

From a short distance away, Bullseye crept over to Nancy and licked her hand, whimpering softly. Then from somewhere down the path he heard his master's urgent voice.

"Bullseye!" called Bill. "This way!"

With a whine the dog sprang to his feet and galloped off in the direction Bill had gone.

"You can't come with me no more, you mangy old cur," Bill said as Bullseye caught up with him and Oliver. "They saw you. They'll watch you now until they find me."

Oliver could see that the big man was sad. He pulled a short crowbar from his pocket and raised it. Bullseye growled. The hair on his neck stood up and he backed away. Bill spoke almost softly.

"Come now, old man," he said. "You aren't scared of me, are you? You aren't afraid of your old Bill."

Bullseye's ears went flat against his head. He growled again and Bill's face grew dark with anger. Raising the crowbar, he swung it suddenly at his dog. But the dog ducked and ran back down the path toward the bridge, yelping with fright.

At the bridge a bargeman was questioning Mr. Brownlow. Had Mr. Brownlow heard anything or seen anyone.

"No," he said sadly. "I wish I had, but it was so dark."

Just then Bullseye appeared at the edge of the group. He sat down, staring warily at the spot where Nancy lay.

"Wait a minute," cried Mr. Brownlow. "That dog! He was here when I found the girl."

"Anyone know whose it is?" asked a seaman.

A mutter rippled through the group. "No," they said. "Never

seen him before. . . . Neither have I."

A second bargeman pushed to the front of the crowd and studied the bewildered dog.

"I know him," he said. "I've seen him at the Three Cripples. Here, boy." He snapped his fingers. "You come along with us."

Someone slipped a rope around Bullseye's neck and, after a moment's hesitation, the dog started off down the street with the crowd behind him.

Out of force of habit, Bullseye headed straight for the Inn of the Three Cripples with the bargeman, Mr. Brownlow, and the others close behind. By the time they reached the tavern there were more than a dozen in the indignant band—including two constables. The boisterous crowd in the inn lapsed immediately into hostile silence when confronted by the well-dressed Mr. Brownlow and the constables. There were many people present who were not at all anxious to meet up with the law.

"Anyone know this dog?" asked one constable.

Cries of "Naw!" and "'Course we don't," rippled through the unfriendly crowd.

"Now you listen here, all of you," snapped the constable. "A young woman's been murdered—maybe you even know her—and the dog was with her."

The crowd at the Three Cripples suddenly became alert. A few looked about the room.

"Was it our Nance?" one whispered.

A burly stevedore stepped forward.

"I know the mutt," he admitted. "It belongs to Sikes."

"Know where he lives?"

The stevedore shook his head and the constable turned once more to the crowd.

"Does *anyone* know where this Sikes fellow lives?" he asked.

165

The crowd was tense. They eyed each other significantly and it was obvious that they had agreed not to talk. The mood had shifted. They weren't unfriendly anymore, but nobody wanted to incur the vicious temper of Bill Sikes.

"Well," said the stevedore at last, "if anyone knows, I bet *he* does."

He pointed at Bullseye, who barked sharply and strained against the rope, trying to reach the door.

CHAPTER 19

Bill Sikes flung open Fagin's door. He shoved Oliver inside, then stepped in himself and slammed the door behind him. The room was dark except for one candle and the light that flickered from the fire in the chimney kitchen. In the dark corners of the loft the boys slept. Fagin, who was kneeling by the fire, quickly replaced the loose floorboard and looked up, startled and fearful.

"Bill," he said. "What's happened? Why have you come here?"

"Brass," Bill panted. "I need some brass!"

Around the room the boys stirred on their sacking beds and began to wake up. They peered uneasily into the dim light. It was easy to see that Fagin was scared.

"What is it?" he said. "What's wrong?"

"The brass!" hissed Bill. "I need cash." He stepped menacingly toward Fagin, entering the circle of light. Fagin stared transfixed as he saw blood on the big man's coat.

"Blood! . . . Bill, are we in trouble?" he gasped. "Where's Nancy?"

"She won't peach on no one no more," muttered Bill.

By now the boys were out of bed, half-dressed and huddling anxiously about the room. They watched as a look of horrified comprehension and terror spread across Fagin's face.

"You didn't!" the old man whispered. "Not Nancy! She'd never have told on you, Bill!"

"She must have," said Bill. "That rich gent was waiting for her at the bridge."

Realizing the danger Fagin suddenly flew into a rage.

"Then why do you come here?" he shrieked. "Are you crazy? Get out of here!"

Bill's knuckles turned white as he gripped the collar of Fagin's robe.

"I told you," he said through clenched teeth. "I want some money."

Hastily Fagin pulled out the leather bag that hung from a cord around his neck. With trembling hands he began fishing out some notes.

"Here," he said. "How much do you want? Ten? Twenty?"

Bill yanked away the bag. "I'll take it all," he hissed. "You owe it to me . . ."

He broke off, cocking his head toward the window and listening. From the streets below came the high-pitched sound of a dog's excited barking. With the exception of Oliver, who sat cowering in a chair, everyone ran to the window and peered out. Far below, coming over the canal bridge, the bobbing lights of torches and lanterns could be seen. In the lead, straining at the end of a rope, was Bullseye.

"It's him!" cried Bill. "They've got Bullseye and he's bringing them here!"

The room was a sudden chaos of movement. "Quick," Fagin barked. "All of you—out the back way. Charlie, get the trap open!"

The Dodger stood lookout at the window.

Charlie and another boy ran quickly to a corner and moved a chest of drawers, revealing a trap door in the floor. Fagin scurried about the room, gathering his treasure box from under the floor and flapping at the boys like a mad hen. Oliver meanwhile had risen to his feet and stood quivering in the center of the room.

169

"Hey!" cried the Dodger from his post at the window. "That old geezer what took Oliver is there. They're all coming here!"

"It's Mr. Brownlow!" Oliver cried. "He's come for me!"

He ran toward the door and plunged headlong into Bill Sikes.

"No you don't," he said. "You're coming with me!"

Fagin stared, dumfounded. "Are you crazy!" he said. "Let him go! You'll only make things worse for all of us."

Bill shook his head. "No," he said. "It's me they're after. But they won't get me—not with the boy alive."

He pulled a rope from the rafters and began coiling it around his waist.

"And keep away from me," he said to Fagin. "I don't want to be seen with any of you—except the brat. They won't touch me as long as I've got the kid."

Considerably relieved to be free of Bill, Fagin now rallied and recovered some of his old style. He shrugged and began ushering the boys through the trap door, patting them on the head as they disappeared down the hidden stairway.

"You're on your own now for a while, boys," he said. "Good luck!"

For the first time, the Dodger seemed unsure of himself.

"What's going to happen to me, Fagin?" he said uncertainly.

Fagin took the boy's face in his long hands. "Live up to your name, old man," he said cheerfully. "Dodge about sharpish. I'll be seeing you again soon enough."

Then, as he lowered the trap door over his own unkempt head, Fagin grinned back at Oliver.

"Be a good boy, Oliver," he said. "We didn't mean to do you no harm."

CHAPTER 20

Though he half wanted to, there was no time for Oliver to bid old Fagin good-by. Before the trap door had fully closed, Bill grabbed Oliver by the shoulder and yanked him out onto the rooftop bridge. Almost directly below them, hurrying up the road, came the constables, Mr. Brownlow, and the ever-growing crowd.

Bullseye stopped in his tracks and began barking furiously at the rooftop bridge.

"It's him!" someone cried. "It's Sikes—and he's got the boy!"

Cursing under his breath, Bill pulled Oliver across the bridge.

173

Below, the crowd followed, reaching the bottom of the sagging stairway that connected the bridge with the street just as the two fugitives reached the top.

"Stand back," shouted a policeman. "We've got him!"

For a split-second Bill glared defiantly down the stairs at the crowd. Then in one movement he kicked in a window next to the stairway and, taking Oliver with him, disappeared inside the building opposite Fagin's loft.

The room in which Oliver and Bill found themselves was the upper floor of a rickety abandoned warehouse. As the two rushed toward a window on the opposite side, Bill hastily tied his rope around Oliver's waist. Just outside the window a heavy pole jutted out over the street. It was a hoist that had been used for lifting goods into the warehouse. Across the street on the same level with Bill and Oliver stood a narrow parapet beyond which stretched a roof. To Bill Sikes it represented safety. Carefully Bill gauged the distance across with his eye. He raised Oliver to the window ledge and commanded him to climb out onto the hoist.

"When you get to the end," he hissed, "tie your end of the rope to the hoist. And tie it tight," he said. "I'm going to swing across on it."

From the stairway came the sounds of the crowd as it neared the broken window where Oliver and Bill had entered the warehouse. Oliver looked back hopefully, but the stairs creaked and began to give way under the great weight of the crowd. Bill grinned as the people cried out in terror and clattered back down into the street.

"Hurry now!" Bill commanded. "Get going!"

Straddling the hoist, Oliver swayed dizzily over the street.

"I can't, Mr. Sikes," he pleaded. "I can't do it."

"You'd better," threatened Bill. "I'm right here waiting for you if you don't. Get out there."

Oliver slowly edged himself out on the hoist. Placing his hands on the pole between his knees he inched himself along until, at last, he was at the end. With one hand he untied the rope around his waist and began, shakily, to tie it to the end of the hoist. Below him a crowd began to gather. They stared silently up, not daring to make a sound which might startle Oliver into falling. At last the rope was tied. At the window, Bill tested the strength of the knot. Then, taking a firm grip on his end of the rope he swung out over the street toward the parapet of the opposite building.

Through the air came a barrage of cobblestones which the men in the street had pried up and were hurling at the big man. A few hit him, but he reached the narrow parapet safely. With a mocking grin, he began loosening the rope around his waist. As he raised his arms to pull the noose over his head, his pistol tumbled from his belt and clattered to the street.

Clinging desperately to the hoist, Oliver watched as a man below dived for the weapon and took aim. The loud crack of the pistol rang out sharply and Oliver stared, sickened, as Bill clutched at his side, staggered momentarily, and fell from the parapet with the rope still around him. The hoist creaked dangerously under Oliver as the weight of Bill's body jerked the rope taut. The ancient hoist was about to give way, when the knot around Bill's waist slipped loose and the man thudded to the street.

For a long time Oliver clung to the hoist, his eyes closed and his mind blank with shock. At last the sound of a kind voice behind him made him look over his shoulder at the window. It was Mr. Brownlow and a constable.

"Keep quite still, Oliver," Mr. Brownlow said gently. "We'll have you down soon. It's all over now."

CHAPTER 21

While Oliver was being rescued, a small figure in a large coat mingled with the dispersing crowd in the street. It was the Artful Dodger up to his old tricks again. Gently raising the coattail of one of the onlookers, he carefully removed a fat leather wallet from the man's hip pocket. Then, realizing suddenly that he was standing beside a constable, he backed quietly out of the crowd and started down the street. From a dark doorway a tall man stepped forward and put a hand on the Dodger's shoulder. The boy started, his face taut with a mixture of fear and feigned innocence.

"Yes, young man," said the stranger. "And do I have the honor of your acquaintance?"

"Oh, Fagin!" said the Dodger. "It's you!"

He laughed with relief, mischievously dangling the wallet in front of Fagin. Fagin raised his hand to cover a cough and the wallet disappeared, leaving only the greedy twinkle of the old man's eyes to tell where it had gone. Momentarily the two stared at each other, shrugging their shoulders and shaking their heads resignedly.

"Same old Dodger," chuckled Fagin.

"Same old Fagin," said the Dodger fondly.

Linking arms, the two friends strode jauntily into the dawning day to round up the other boys and get the establishment back into operation.

The soft clip-clopping of a horse and the squeaking of carriage wheels did not disturb the early morning stillness of Bloomsbury Square. Peeping over the white houses, the sun had not yet dried a drop of dew on the green, but lit only the top of the large tree behind which Bill and Nancy had hidden on the day of Oliver's kidnaping. The driver of the carriage muttered a "whoa there," to the horse which snorted softly and halted before the Brownlow house. Inside the carriage Oliver slept soundly. Mr. Brownlow stepped quietly to the street, lifted the boy in his arms, and smiled up at Mrs. Bedwin who was peering anxiously out of a top floor window. The kind woman disappeared at once and a moment later flung open the front door, her face wet with tearful joy.

"Oh, Mr. Brownlow," she cried, "you *did* find him! I was so worried, but you found him after all. I'm so glad. Praise be! I'm so glad!"

She placed her hand on Oliver's forehead and smoothed back

his hair. The boy opened his eyes and, as Mr. Brownlow set him down, he hugged the big woman tightly.

"Welcome home, Oliver," said Mr. Brownlow, leading his family inside.

The door to the big house closed and Bloomsbury Square was still once more—except now for the chirping of the birds in the old green tree and the sweet voice of the flower girl singing, "Who will buy?"